Praise for
John D. MacDonald

"MacDonald isn't simply popular; he's also good."

—ROGER EBERT

"MacDonald's books are narcotic and, once hooked, a reader can't kick the habit until the supply runs out."

—*Chicago Tribune Book World*

"John D. MacDonald remains one of my idols."

—DONALD WESTLAKE

"The Dickens of mid-century America—popular, prolific and ... conscience-ridden about his environment. ... A thoroughly American author."   —*The Boston Globe*

"It will be for his crisply written, smoothly plotted mysteries that MacDonald will be remembered."   —*USA Today*

"MacDonald had the marvelous ability to create attention-getting characters who doubled as social critics. In MacDonald novels, it is the rule rather than the exception to find, in the midst of violence and mayhem, a sentence, a paragraph, or several pages of rumination on love, morality, religion, architecture, politics, business, the general state of the world or of Florida."   —*Sarasota Herald-Tribune*

By John D. MacDonald

The Brass Cupcake
Murder for the Bride
Judge Me Not
Wine for the Dreamers
Ballroom of the Skies
The Damned
Dead Low Tide
The Neon Jungle
Cancel All Our Vows
All These Condemned
Area of Suspicion
Contrary Pleasure
A Bullet for Cinderella
Cry Hard, Cry Fast
You Live Once
April Evil
Border Town Girl
Murder in the Wind
Death Trap
The Price of Murder
The Empty Trap
A Man of Affairs
The Deceivers
Clemmie
Cape Fear (The Executioners)
Soft Touch
Deadly Welcome

Please Write for Details
The Crossroads
The Beach Girls
Slam the Big Door
The End of the Night
The Only Girl in the Game
Where Is Janice Gantry?
One Monday We Killed Them All
A Key to the Suite
A Flash of Green
The Girl, the Gold Watch
 & Everything
On the Run
The Drowner
The House Guest
End of the Tiger and Other Stories
The Last One Left
S*E*V*E*N
Condominium
Other Times, Other Worlds
Nothing Can Go Wrong
The Good Old Stuff
One More Sunday
More Good Old Stuff
Barrier Island
A Friendship: The Letters of Dan Rowan
 and John D. MacDonald, 1967–1974

THE TRAVIS MCGEE SERIES

The Deep Blue Good-by
Nightmare in Pink
A Purple Place for Dying
The Quick Red Fox
A Deadly Shade of Gold
Bright Orange for the Shroud
Darker Than Amber
One Fearful Yellow Eye
Pale Gray for Guilt
The Girl in the Plain
 Brown Wrapper
Dress Her in Indigo

The Long Lavender Look
A Tan and Sandy Silence
The Scarlet Ruse
The Turquoise Lament
The Dreadful Lemon Sky
The Empty Copper Sea
The Green Ripper
Free Fall in Crimson
Cinnamon Skin
The Lonely Silver Rain

The Official Travis McGee Quizbook

DEAD
LOW TIDE

DEAD LOW TIDE

A NOVEL

John D. MacDonald

RANDOM HOUSE TRADE PAPERBACKS

NEW YORK

2014 Random House Trade Paperback Edition

Published in the United States by Random House Trade Paperbacks,
an imprint of Random House, a division of Random House LLC,
a Penguin Random House Company, New York.

RANDOM HOUSE and the HOUSE colophon
are registered trademarks of Random House LLC.

Originally published in paperback in the United States by Fawcett,
an imprint of Random House, a division of Random House LLC, in 1953.

ISBN 978-0-8129-8420-0
eBook ISBN 978-0-307-82705-0

www.atrandom.com

Book design by Christopher M. Zucker

The Singular John D. MacDonald

Dean Koontz

WHEN I WAS IN COLLEGE, I had a friend, Harry Record, who was smart, funny, and a demon card player. Harry was a successful history major, while I passed more time playing pinochle than I spent in class. For the three and a half years that I required to graduate, I heard Harry rave about this writer named John D. MacDonald, "John D" to his most ardent readers. Of the two of us, Harry was the better card player and just generally the cooler one. Consequently, I was protective of my position, as an English major, to be the better judge of literature, don't you know. I remained reluctant to give John D a look.

Having read mostly science fiction, I found many of my professors' assigned authors markedly less exciting than Robert Heinlein and Theodore Sturgeon, but I was determined to read the right thing. For every Flannery O'Connor whose work I could race through with delight, there were three like Virginia Woolf, who made me want to throw their books off a high cliff and leap after them. Nevertheless, I continued to shun Harry's beloved John D.

Five or six years after college, I was a full-time writer with numerous credits in science fiction, struggling to move into suspense and mainstream work. I was making progress but not fast enough to suit me. By now I knew that John D was widely admired, and I finally sat down with one of his books. In the next thirty days, I read thirty-four of them. The singular voice and style of the man overwhelmed me, and the next novel I wrote was such an embarrassingly slavish imitation of a MacDonald tale that I had to throw away the manuscript.

I apologized to Harry for doubting him. He was so pleased to hear me proclaiming the joys of John D that he only said "I told you so" on, oh, twenty or thirty occasions.

Over the years, I have read every novel by John D at least three times, some of them twice that often. His ability to evoke a time and place—mostly Florida but also the industrial Midwest, Las Vegas, and elsewhere—was wonderful, and he could get inside an occupation to give you the details and the feel of it like few other writers I've ever read. His pacing was superb, the flow of his prose irresistible, and his suspense watch-spring tight.

Of all his manifest strengths as a writer, however, I am most in awe of his ability to create characters who are as real as anyone I've met in life. John D sometimes paused in the headlong rush of his story to spin out pages of background on a character. At first when this happened, I grumbled about getting on with the story. But I soon discovered that he could make the character so fascinating that when the story began to race forward again, I wanted it to slow down so I could learn more about this person who so intrigued and/or delighted me. There have been many good suspense novelists in recent decades, but in my experience, none has produced characters with as much humanity and truth as those in Mac-Donald's work.

Like most who have found this author, I am an admirer of his Travis McGee series, which features a first-person narrator as good as any in the history of suspense fiction and better than most. But I love the standalone novels even more. *Cry Hard, Cry Fast. Where Is Janice Gantry? The Last One Left. A Key to the Suite. The Drowner. The Damned. A Bullet for Cinderella. The Only Girl in the Game. The Crossroads. All These Condemned.* Those are not my only favorites, just a few of them, and many deal with interesting businesses and occupations. Mr. MacDonald's work gives the reader deep and abiding pleasure for many reasons, not the least of which is that it portrays the contemporary life of his day with as much grace and fidelity as any writer of the period, and thus it also provides compelling social history.

In 1985, when my publisher, Putnam, wanted to send advance proof copies of *Strangers* to Mr. MacDonald among others, I literally grew shaky at the thought of him reading it. I suggested that they shouldn't send it to him, that, as famous and prolific as he was, the proof would be an imposition on him; in truth, I feared that he would find the novel unsatisfying. Putnam sent it to him anyway, and he gave us an enthusiastic endorsement. In addition, he wrote to me separately, in an avuncular tone, kindly advising me how to avoid some of the pitfalls of the publishing business, and he wrote to my publisher asking her to please carefully consider the packaging of the book and not condemn it to the horror genre. She more or less condemned it to the genre anyway, but I took his advice to heart.

In my experience, John D. MacDonald, the man, was as kind and thoughtful as his fiction would lead you to believe that he must be. That a writer's work accurately reflects his soul is a rarer thing than you might imagine, but in his case, the reflection is clear and true. For that reason, it has been a special honor, in fact a grace, to be asked to write this introduction.

Reader, prepare to be enchanted by the books of John D. MacDonald. And Harry, I am not as much of an idiot as I was in years gone by—though I know you won't let me get away with claiming not to be to any degree an idiot anymore.

DEAD
LOW TIDE

One

I WORKED PRETTY LATE on the estimate. The lady wanted to know how much the ten-unit motel was going to cost her, and John Long, my boss, had worked on her, so of course nobody else in the world could possibly put it up except John Long, Contractors. She already had her piece of land fronting on the Tamiami Trail, and it was September, and she wanted the motel up before the season began and the tourists started wandering around with money falling out of their pockets.

It was September, like I said, and hotter than hell's hinges, so my fingers left smudges on the paper and sweat rolled down my bare chest, and all I wanted in the world was to get finished and put the top down on the car and drive thirty miles to Sarasota and sit in a booth in line with the air conditioning and have Red bring me a Mule, which I would drink with my hand around the chilled copper, while Charlie

Davies played "Body and Soul" for me. I was fed up with John Long, and tired of making estimates without either the proper knowledge or experience, and weary with chasing around after cement here and cinder blocks there and cull cypress the next place. John Long had given me the big talk about opportunity, so rich it left my eyes glazed, so I'd started in the office, answering the phone and typing on two fingers. A year of it and I still answered the phone, typed on four fingers, and made estimates and chased materials and got twenty bucks more a week than a year ago.

Gordy Brogan and Big Dake were the foremen and one of them would handle this job, this motel, for the lady, while John Long went ahead with his Key Estates. And if the lady got restless, somebody would tell John and he'd come down in the Cadillac and bellow at the crew for twenty minutes, and give the lady that big ripe boyish grin and that would keep her happy for a couple of weeks, because he could do that with just the grin, and knowing when and how to use it. And I knew that if any profit came out of the motel it would go right into Key Estates, because that was where John Long had decided he would make the killing he'd waited for.

Anyway, my eyes had slowly got unglazed, and I had got lately into the habit of talking to myself in a most formal fashion. "Andrew Hale McClintock, exactly what in hell are you doing here?"

For the kind of building she wanted, it was a case of multiplying out the square footage and multiplying that by a cost factor which John Long had decided would give him a decent profit margin, then figuring the extras, and then rounding the total off to the next highest round number. Then there was a kid John knew who was working in a grocery store and taking a correspondence course in architecture. Given the working drawings, he would whip up a drawing of a front elevation that would look pretty, professional, and very impressive. John gave him ten bucks apiece for those drawings.

It got so dark I had to turn on the fluorescent desk lamp, and it seemed to make the room hotter. When the door clacked shut behind me I lifted about six inches off the chair, since I hadn't heard it open. I turned but I couldn't see well into the darkness because of the white glare of lamp on the paper I had been working on.

She came closer and I saw that it was Mrs. John Long. I jumped up and grabbed for my shirt, and she said, "No, don't bother. It's too hot in here for a shirt, Andy."

John had introduced me to her after I had gone to work for him. I would see her in the office once in a while, and we would nod and show our teeth, and I had seen her around town at sundry civic functions and those places of entertainment where the common people mingled with the gentry. I kept seeing her picture in the paper, for charity drives and things going on at the Beach Club and all that sort of thing. She is one of those dark-haired Alabama girls, a kind of a stringy little girl, dark, and, if you look closely, feature by feature, you can see that she is not pretty. But her face is so alive all the time that afterward you would swear she is pretty. There are no kids, and I would say she is thirty, to John's forty.

She sat down in a chair near my desk, sat down a bit heavy and tired. She had on a sort of blue denim play suit thing, and she slouched in the chair and crossed her thin brown legs and asked for a cigarette. Her face was in shadow, and when I held the light for her I saw her face looked sort of dulled. It wasn't alive, the way I had always seen it before, and there wasn't much lilt in her voice.

She said, "I was driving around, going no place, and I saw the light. I sure hope I haven't kept you from finishing something, Andy." Always before, it had been Mr. McClintock. Maybe guys without shirts revert to first names.

"I just finished," I lied. It didn't seem in character for Mrs. John Long to be driving around doing nothing. According to the papers she couldn't have too many free minutes in a day.

"Do you like working here, Andy?"

"I like it fine, Mrs. Long."

"How did you happen to land here, Andy?"

I wondered if she was spending a hot evening improving employee morale, by getting the serf to talk about himself. "I answered an ad in the paper."

"I mean before."

"The whole history?"

"Andy, don't you sound so all bristly now. I really want to know."

The appearance of genuine interest always seems to soothe us. "Well, Mrs. Long, I graduated from Syracuse University three years ago. Business Administration."

"Only three years out of college?"

"I was an old college boy. The class called me 'Daddy.' I'm twenty-eight now. A war got in the way of my education. Anyway, I went to work for a big corporation in Buffalo. I found out that made me nervous. It was just too big. It was like a special form of social security. All I had to do was keep my hair combed for thirty years and get myself retired. So I saved some money, took off like a bird, and came down here to the Land of Opportunity. The New Frontier."

"Any girl, Andy?"

"You're getting quite a dossier, Mrs. Long. They come and go. I cook pretty good, and I'm pure hell at pressing a pair of pants."

"I've wondered about you."

"Why, Mrs. Long?"

"You call me Mary Eleanor, hear? That Mrs. Long makes me feel awful old."

"O.K., Mary Eleanor." The southland seems to insist on giving the ladies two names. "Why were you wondering about me?"

"I don't know, for certain. John has always had such little old dumb ugly people in the office. And you're big and nice looking and smart. But he doesn't pay much, I guess. So I—"

"Mrs.—Mary Eleanor, just what have you got on your mind? We're having a nice visit, but what do you want?"

"It's awful darn hot in here, Andy. If you're finished up like you say, come on for a ride."

The last thing I wanted to do was go for any rides with the boss's wife. That's frowned on in schools of business administration. Bosses' daughters they approve of—not wives. Something was chewing on Mary Eleanor, and she didn't want to come right out with it. I know now that if my heap, my old Chevy convertible, had been parked out in front instead of being incarcerated in Gadgkin's Repair Garage for an overdue ring job, I would have pleaded a date. But it was a hot night, and I was carless, and perhaps careless. The vehicle would save me a hike to the bus stop, and another hike down my road. And, as another extenuating circumstance, I had my shirt off and I was getting fatly weary of John Long and unfulfilled promises, and what was this anyway—the Middle

Ages? Can't the boss's young wife give me a lift? And if something was chewing on her, wasn't it a good deed?

"Tell you what, Mary Eleanor, I would dearly appreciate a lift home. Wait a minute while I do some sorting."

She sat quietly while I shuffled the papers and put them in the desk drawer. I stood up and put on my shirt, reached over and snapped out the desk light. Streetlights came through the big front window. Day or night, that office is a goldfish bowl. Her little black MG was parked forty feet away, with the top down. She swung ahead of me and got behind the wheel and I got in beside her.

"I live at that Shady Grove Retreat place," I said.

"I know."

I'd seen her go by in that little jet car, but this new viewpoint was more distressing. Anything in the road ahead of her was a personal challenge. She went scooting up the trail. I opened my mouth when we were a quarter mile from the turnoff, but we were by it before I could even say "Hey." I concentrated all my efforts on trying to act relaxed. We were five miles up the trail in something less than five minutes. She slowed for a patch of neon that was rushing at us, slewed into the parking area, skidded the back end, and parked with the hood shoved halfway into a flowering bush.

"I don't live here, Mary Eleanor," I said, only a bit faintly.

"You can have a drink with me, can't you?" she said as she got out. She walked toward the door of the place. It would be a bit fantastic, I decided, to sit out in the car and sulk. I began to realize why girls carry mad money. I untangled myself from the MG and followed along. As I walked behind her I became aware that in spite of her being a scrawny type, she wagged very pleasantly and cutely in the blue demin outfit, giving me a sort of vague suicidal hope that this was one of those tabloid jobs where the boss's young wife picks a playmate out of the office. I unloaded that notion quickly. Considering the size of the town, and what John Long measured around the forearms, if she started to nibble at me I was going right up a palm tree and squat in the top with the rats.

We got to the door at the same time, and I reached around her and pulled the screen open. I wondered who would be in the place, and I tried to figure out what kind of expression I ought to wear. Business-like, perhaps. A beer-joint conference on matters of great moment.

We went in. Some fans were humming. I gave a self-conscious, "Yo" to a couple of commercial fishermen I knew. There was a creepy blonde singing drunky music at the bar. The owner-manager-bartender seemed to recognize Mary Eleanor, as she got a large hello, but he took a half hitch in his eyebrow as he looked at me, which didn't please me since I have paid him beer money as good as anybody's. It then occurred to me that, nibble or no, just being seen with her wasn't the happiest way to spend an evening.

Mary Eleanor went crisply down to the very last booth in sort of an alcove across from the door of the ladies' room. I put up the window and the fans made some of the night air move in across our faces, so it wasn't bad.

Owner-manager-bartender waddled back and took her order for bourbon and water on the side, and mine for a bottle of Miller's. As soon as he went away she dug in a small white purse and took out a ten and pushed it across at me.

"I can handle it," I said, maybe a bit on the stuffy side.

"Please, Andy. Or I won't enjoy my drink."

"Dutch, then."

She nodded. It was the first time I'd ever had a good chance to look at her face. Big bright black eyes, and just a shade too much in the tooth department, so she had a very faint look of coming out of one of Disney's woodland dells. She had a little mesh of wrinkles at the corners of her eyes, and her underlip was about three times the thickness of the one on top. Her ears were little and they grew flat to her head. Her hands were small, with spidery fingers and sort of lumpy knuckles. But, all in all, I would say, an attractive item. First you saw the thin look, and then you saw that her breasts looked high and sharp, and as I have mentioned, there was a nice side to side wave of the seat of the blue denim as you happened to walk behind her. I guess I was giving it too close a study. It leaned back in the booth.

"Andy—I went over everyone, thinking, and you're the only . . ."

The drinks came then and she shut up. They were on a pay-as-you-go deal, so he took the ten and brought the change back. By the time he got back with it, her shot of bourbon was gone, and so was one sip of the water, and she pushed the shot glass toward him. He picked it up and went off with it.

The interruption had given her time to think that maybe there was a better way of edging up on the subject, but I was beginning to think I was a little too placid about the whole thing, and a little loss of balance wouldn't hurt, so I said, "The only what?"

"What? Oh—the only one who's usually in the office."

You don't call your boss's wife a liar, even when she is. The new shot came and she was still holding it, rim-full, rock steady, when the change came back. She threw it down with a hard toss, and one ripple of her throat, and took a little sip of water. They do something to those little dark girls. Maybe it's a special course at Sweet Briar. All night they can drink, and nothing happens. Plying them with same is bad technique, because whatever happens, it happens to you, and they take you home and in the morning your head rattles like a broken transmission.

"What do you want, Mary Eleanor?"

"I just plain don't know how to ask you, Andy."

"Try English."

"All right. Will you find out something for me? Will you find out what's wrong with John?"

"Wrong? Offhand the only thing wrong with your husband is that he wears a size nineteen collar and he could probably run a hundred yards in eleven seconds with one of me tucked under each arm, and I weigh one eighty. Oh, yes, and you can't pin him down. That I know. Ask him if tomorrow is Tuesday and he bangs you on the shoulder and asks you if you had a good old time last Sunday."

She smiled, and this was a smile not for the society section of our daily newspaper. It was more the sort of smile you wear to get your lips out of the way so you can examine a loose filling. "Oh, I know how hard it is to make him tell you anything, Andy. Whatever it is, it's bad."

"What's bad?"

"Whatever it is that's wrong. He sits and his eyes look right through things and he doesn't hear me. He groans something awful in his sleep, and the other night there he was, sitting right up in bed and making a real high thin screaming sound like a woman. When I ask him what is wrong, he goes off someplace and closes the door real quiet.

And he gets up in the night and walks around and around our house, and once I came home and I didn't know he was there and I came in quiet like, and he was sitting there all by himself, crying without making any noise."

"I think I fell off a curve back there, Mrs. Long. You want *me* to snuffle around your husband?"

"Oh, I could hire somebody, maybe, who does that for a living, you know, from Tampa or Miami or someplace, but that would be an outsider, and I thought somebody who was sort of—in the family. I mean you're like—like the license on his car. He looks at it every day, but he doesn't really see it."

"Thank you too much."

"You know I don't mean it that way, Andy."

"Look. I work for the guy. At the moment, quite frankly, I happen to be a little sore at him. He hasn't come through on what he promised me originally. I'll tell you that much. If he has business troubles, I don't know what they are. If he has emotional problems, it would seem to me that's your affair, not mine. You're his wife. Ask him what's bothering him."

"But I have! And he won't tell me. Wouldn't you say this is my duty, to find out what's wrong so that I can help?"

"Not through me, you don't."

"I just don't really see why you get so damn huffy about it. After all, I'm not asking you to steal anything."

"Maybe I just don't have the conspiratorial temperament. Sorry."

The tears which I had been half expecting appeared. They swelled fat on the edge of the lower lids and broke over and ran down, and the one from the left eye got way down to the corner of her mouth before the quick sharp tongue-tip slanted over and caught it.

"But I love him so much, Andy, and he's in trouble and he won't tell me what it is, and so how can I help him if I don't know what it is. Please, Andy?"

"Look, Mary Eleanor. It's out of my line. Anyway, what could I do? He spends all his time now at Key Estates. That's his baby. He's riding it hard and hustling his own materials, and I have about as much reason to go barging out there as I have to take a fast look at the other side of the moon."

"You could *make* reasons."

"Feeble ones. No. I want to be friends, Mary Eleanor, and in some funny way maybe this flatters me a little, but no dice."

I watched her and saw her slowly accept the idea of the turndown. The noises she'd been making, like a small muffled butter churn, faded away. She blotted the tears, hitched her shoulders, looked out the window.

"No hard feelings?" I asked.

"I guess not, Andy. But it's terrible not to *know*. I just can't *imagine*. He's changing so fast!" Under stress the magnolia accent really ripened. "Can't" came out "kay-yunt" and "fast" turned into "fay-yust."

When they're really magnolia they have a funny way of making me feel a little self-conscious and guilty about being a "noth-run bo-wee." As if I had sharp edges. As if they all come from some isle where they talk to each other in those soft voices, and they live in a place where things are warmer and sweeter and tenderer, and they have a code that is so deep and so much a part of the way they act and behave that they don't ever have to think about it as such. And that, I am afraid, is exactly the way it is with them. It makes you feel a bit cold, angular, displaced. She had lifted the edge of the code just enough so I could see in—see trouble and tears, and letting me look in was, in itself, a violation of the code.

But, in my own way, I had a code of my own, and I could not see myself creepy-mousing around, trying to find out what gnawed the soul of my employer.

"I guess I understand, Andy. But, please, promise me one thing. If you should happen—well, sort of by accident, to find out what it is, you'll let me know."

"If it's the sort of thing you should know. And if he isn't telling you, he's made that decision already, hasn't he?"

"You get so darn logical like, Andy."

But she managed a faint smile as she said it. Twenty minutes later I stood by my house and watched her horse the black MG off into the night. Funny about her. I hadn't thought there was much to her. But be with her for a little while and you had an idea of just what John Long had for himself. A hundred and three pounds of fire and intensity and aliveness. A little wife that would sing in your blood like chronic malaria. Something to hurry home to when the nights get cool. It is indeed a depressing line of thought for a bachelor. Like a man in a rowboat looking at a cabin cruiser and saying to himself, "By God, I could own one of those if I weren't so damn lazy that I hate the thought of the up-keep."

And I heard the faint crunch of shells as somebody came walking down the road toward my place. I knew who it was. As Mary Eleanor had driven down the road her headlights had swung across a pair of bare brown legs belonging to a gal sitting on some dark steps.

Two

AT THE SOUTH EDGE of town there is a deep narrow
creek which runs into the bay. It is a place where, in season,
the snook gather and respond readily to a yellow buck-tail
dude jerked past their undershot jaws. If you shill a grand-
daddy snook into chomping on same, he will delight to
sprain your wrist. It was there, on the jungly north bank of
the creek that my landlady, Mrs. Elly Tickler, an elfin and
fiftyish widow, built on the general lines of a silo, put up ten
cabins prior to Florida's current glass brick, wrought iron,
and window wall era. They are little bastard-Spanish houses,
with narrow windows, thick walls, and doodads around the
top. They are scattered around the little jungly patch as
though placed by some mystic who used a forked wand. The
result is a pleasant privacy. We all have individual little terraces. There is no attempt at growing a lawn. We have our

crop of sand spurs, sea grapes, castor bean plants, punk trees, and poison ivy, and we all like it fine.

Elly gigglingly admits she is as lazy as a hog in August, and it makes her nervous with people moving in and moving out, so she is delighted to rent to us locals because she can leave us alone and we stay put, even if her income is thereby reduced. In September, particularly, we all experiment with evil-smelling sprays, lotions, and repellents, and Ardy Fowler will tell you, his blue carpenter's eyes as solemn as a reading of the minutes, that it was on the eighth of September three years ago that a flock of mosquitoes carried him thirty feet out over the bay before they got wing-weary and dropped him on an oyster bar. And Andy will even roll up his pants leg and show you the scar where he hit the shells.

So I heard Christy Hallowell come swinging down the road, and heard her stop and slap lustily.

"Donating blood?" I asked her.

She came up to me. "I was about to give you up, McClintock. Until one of your women brought you home. Smell me. This is new stuff and it's working."

"Hmm," I said. "There's carbolic in it. And banana oil. And something else. Pretty elusive, though. Got it! Swamp water. Christy, you smell like an Arabian veterinary."

"Poo. I told you it works. It's called Ray-pell. How was your date?"

"Lush. That was the boss's wife. And now I've got another date with a hunk of cheese. Have some?"

Mosquitoes were clustered around my front door. We scampered in, flailing our arms. Nobody ever locks anything at Tickler Terrace—which is what we call it despite Elly's sign proclaiming that this is Shady Grove Retreat. I got the lights on, gathered up my bug bomb, and disconcerted a few stilt-legged citizens perched on my walls, waiting for sleep and dark, and blood and me.

Christy walked around with me and pointed out a few I had missed, and then she sat on my kitchen table and looked around, and said, "God, you're neat! For a man, I mean. Dusty in spots, but neat."

"We old bachelors, you know. Everything in its place. System, order, efficiency." I opened the refrigerator. "Cheese? Guaranteed to climb on the plate by itself."

"Delightful. Please. And with some of that beer I can see from here. In the can."

I opened her beer and gave it to her, halved the hunk of cheese, poured myself a glass of milk, and sat down at the kitchen table and stared disapprovingly at the round brown knees a foot from my milk. "You have those well greased, my love."

"You're a delicate type, aren't you? Ray-pell does not smell that bad." She got up and walked around and sat down across from me.

I approve of Christy. She's a big brown slim-waisted blonde with a sturdy frame, extra-long legs, a face a bit too round for beauty, with the eyes being the best part. Eyes the shade of wine vinegar.

She is a Midwest blonde and she is something they seem to be growing out there these last few years. Big girls who look smooth and tight and well fitted into their skin. Out there when three of them come down the sidewalk abreast there is something overpowering about them, and you feel that your masculine ego is being hemmed in by a thicket of long, long legs. And they all seem to have an odd, casual lack of any physical self-consciousness. Their splendid bodies are not something to be aware of. Just something they want to keep clean, tanned, and at the proper temperature. When Christy has a day off from Wilburt's Book Nook (books, stationery, office supplies, art supplies, craft supplies, souvenirs, home-made candy and hand-painted neckties), and on the weekends, her approach to holiday is to relax thoroughly, and also she will put on very short shorts and make them shorter by rolling them. And she will put on a very narrow halter and make it narrower by folding in the top and bottom, presenting a disconcerting area of smooth tan hide. When Ardy Fowler sees her coming thusly attired, he will trot into his house and bang the door behind him, though he is quite avuncular when she is dressed. Christy told me solemnly a while back that she thinks Ardy is moody. Ardy told me that it is merely caution.

If you think about those girls they are growing out there in the Midwest, and think about the way they act, and think of how they give an impression of being unused and waiting for something, it can begin to worry you. If nature is planning on setting up a matriarchy, it is only reasonable that the first step is to start developing the shock troops. Any one of them could swing a mace.

Anyway, she talks through her nose, and she made a real messy marriage, and she came to Florida by bus with three hundred dollars in her purse and earned herself a divorce. She hasn't told me much about the guy. She has only mentioned him a couple of times. And each time she had to shut up, because she said that even thinking about him made her stomach swing the way it does when you look into an open wound. Having no special place to go back to, she kept her job at Wilburt's, and though she looks with a frigid eye on the idea of another emotional entanglement, I suspect she will end up being an effective and heart-warming wife for some character who is wandering around not realizing how lucky he is going to be. A few months back, due probably to what April in Florida can do even to a statue in the park, and due to mutual loneliness, and the more functional aspects of need, and due to a niggling, drifting discontent, Christy and I had a brief and rather pointless affair which sneaked up on us when she changed the stinger receipt one blue Sunday dusk.

It did not take us long to find that due to the rather limited emotional involvement we could attain, there was more profit to both of us in friendship than in love with a small *l*, and if we kept on, we would never get back to friendship. Fortunately we quit in time, and without complications. It was just something that had happened, and it wasn't important only in that it probably had to happen, even if only out of curiosity, and we were done with it, and perhaps closer because of it. Closer without antagonism. And it left, me, at least, with one large good memory of lying in bed and sharing one cigarette between us, and laughing so hard about some damn fool thing I have forgotten that tears were running right down Christy's round cheeks and she couldn't catch her breath, and the slant of late afternoon sunlight across us made her look as though she had been fashioned of smooth warm molten gold.

I knew from the way she acted, waiting for me, and coming to eat my cheese, that she had had one of those days, one of those moods. Some people, I'm told, can live alone and fold the walls around themselves and make a snug little box in which they can lie, furry and warm, and sing to themselves and tell stories to themselves about how sweet and wonderful it is to be utterly alone. But our walls are paper, and the sounds of life come through, and sometimes these sounds get Christy down, and sometimes they get me down, and then it is a fine thing to lean, just a little, on somebody who has the same disease, so you don't have to answer questions about symptoms.

We ate our cheese and drank our milk and beer, and I told her about my secret mission, and how I had turned it down. She was intrigued, as she had listened too often, perhaps, to my recent gripes about the job. And it seems as if there never was a woman who did not get pretty feverish about dark secrets. She made some excellent suggestions about how I could have taken the mission and planted a tape recorder in John's hind pocket, and rented a bloodhound, and vacuumed his clothes for that telltale trace of talcum. I told her I didn't know what I'd do without her. At least the subject had taken her out of her mood. She acted better.

One of the florid September rains came along and began to make dice-box sounds in the palm fronds. She jumped up and ran for the front door, but by the time she got there the rain had started to come down like somebody emptying a bucket of fish. We stood and looked out at the wet dark noisy night, feeling the sudden pleasant coolness.

"Off to my bed, McClintock," she said.

"In that? Listen." I listened with her. The hard sound faded, left us in a dripping silence, and the rain roared off down the bay shore like a departing freight train.

The world dripped. She gave me a slightly wry face, and I put my arm around her. She turned quietly, meekly, gratefully into my arms like a small girl, not like five-nine and a hundred and fifty pounds of the pride of the Midwest. She rubbed her forehead against my cheekbone and sighed. Comfort from friends.

I kissed her beside the eye, and said, "God, you're sticky!"

"Ray-pell," she said. She tilted her mouth up and I kissed it. A light, good-night kiss, and I patted the seat of her snugly tailored shorts. We felt, in that dark hall, the little shifting changes of awareness, so we broke it up. We were aware of what could sneak up on us, and we were out of the market, so we broke it up a bit gingerly and carefully. The way a fat man on a diet will hide the temptation on the menu with his thumb while he orders Ry-Krisp.

She swung her long brown legs down my steps and out my short path to the road and she was gone before I heard her call back, "Thanks for the cheese, McClintock. It reeked."

I went back in, stalked new arrivals with my bomb, cleaned up the kitchen, showered long and cold and well, folded down the light spread on my bed, climbed into it, covered one third of myself with the sheet, picked up my book, and read myself into semiconsciousness. With the light off, I thought for a little while about Mary Eleanor and remembered I could pick up my car before work and wondered what was eating John Long, and thought about Christy, two hundred feet away, across the night, doubtless covered, also, by a corner of a sheet.

Three

BY TEN-FIFTEEN the next morning, Thursday morning, I had the lady's estimate reasonably neatly typed, and her ten-unit court was going to cost her fifty-six thousand dollars. I guessed she'd paid ten for the land. And it would cost her at least fourteen in equipment and extras. Eighty thousand on the hook, and I hoped the lady realized that eighty thousand, say at five per cent, brings in four thousand a year all by its little self, without aid and benefit of twenty beds a day to make during the season. I hoped she realized that first she had to make that four thousand, and then she had to make enough to cover running expenses and overhead and depreciation, and if she could make anything at all over that, it was found money. The second owner, who would probably get the whole works for fifty thousand, would probably be shrewd enough to know what he was doing. The lady had multiplied ten rooms by ten dollars a room and multiplied a hundred dollars a night by three hundred and sixty-five, and dreamed of Cadillacs and fast boats.

I was depressing myself, and it was a sticky day. Feeble excuse number one. Take the estimate out to John, I told myself. So I locked the office, got in the car, and went out to Key Estates.

Florida, particularly along the west coast, all the way from Cedar Keys to the careful monied smell of Naples, is constantly growing—not in the normal fashion of other places, with more houses going up on existing land, but the land itself is growing. Shaggy dredges park in the bay flats, snarling and wheezing as they suck up mud and guck and shells and small unwary fish. The debris is piled moistly and it stinks for a time, then whitens in the sun. It is leveled and stamped down and then houses go up on it so fast they seem to appear with a small clinking sound—the way Walt Disney grows flowers.

People who bought water-front land and admired their view of the bay find themselves three blocks inland. Incantations are said, in which strange words appear. Riparian rights is a good word. It sounds stentorian and nobody knows exactly what it means. It means turning water into land and putting houses on it. And standard procedure, along with the houses, is to stuff some palm trees into the made land. They have a nasty habit of taking a long time to die, so you can usually sell the house before the palm turns to a rich tobacco brown. Also, you have to have a sea wall, or the bay will reclaim its own. And you put about seven-eighths of an inch of topsoil on the shells and plant rye grass And a hedge of Australian pine that grows so fast you can hear it.

And you pray, every night, that the big one doesn't come

this year. A big one stomped and churned around Cedar Keys a couple of years back, and took a mild pass at Clearwater and huffed itself out. One year it is going to show up, walking out of the Gulf and up the coast, like a big red top walking across the schoolyard. And the wind isn't going to mess things up too much, because people have learned what to do about the wind. But that water is going to have real fun with the made land, with the sea walls and packed shells and the thin topsoil. It's going to be like taking a good kick at an anthill, and then the local segment of that peculiar aberration called the human race is going to pick itself up, whistle for the dredges, and start it all over again.

Our key, which is narrow and seven miles long, gives us plenty of bay, plenty of mullet, and two good fishing bridges. It's called Horseshoe Key, and there are three schools of thought about the name. One group insists it comes from Horseshoe Crabs, and a second insists that one part of it once was shaped like a horseshoe, and the loudest segment of all insists on a myth concerning one Daddy Morgan who first lived on the key in a shack and got himself kicked to death.

At any rate, it is seven miles long and the gulf tides keep changing the sand shapes at the ends of it, and if you happen to own two hundred feet of it—extending from the central road down the middle of the key to the gulf beach—then you can be particularly content because your piece, two hundred by four hundred, is worth twenty-five thousand bucks at going rates. And if you bought it in '34, you paid about two hundred and fifty to three hundred dollars for it, and that will make you very unhappy that you didn't buy a thousand feet, but you can still sneer gently and happily at the dullards who neglected to buy any. Now, if your two-hundred-foot chunk should run from Horseshoe Drive east to the bay, you are not precisely as happy because in that event your land is only worth eleven thousand—but then, you could have picked that up for sixty dollars in '34.

John Long bought his fifteen hundred feet of bay frontage running through to Horseshoe Drive for ten thousand dollars in 1943. I know because I looked it up at the courthouse. Which makes it worth, at going rates, eighty-two thousand, five hundred dollars.

Herewith, for the benefit of those who like to think about money, I present the mathematics of made land. John Long started with fifteen hundred feet of bay front worth fifty-five dollars a foot. He had riparian rights to fill out as far as the inland waterways channel some nine hundred feet out in the bay. So he had the dredge make him a long finger of land three hundred feet wide, stretching from his property out to the channel. That left him with just twelve hundred of his original fifteen hundred feet of land. But, measuring the shoreline of the finger he built, he got his three hundred right back, plus eighteen hundred more. So he not only ended up with thirty-three hundred feet of water front, worth a total of a hundred and eighty-one thousand, five hundred, but, in the process, the dredge mooched out a private channel very handy for the boats of the people who would live in the houses on the made land. Dredges and sea walls are expensive, but on a quantity operation like John Long's he got more land value back than he put out.

Then, with a drag line setup, he ran the new channel right back into the heart of the original property. That made interior lots more desirable, and also provided a nice topping to spread over the new finger. Out on Horseshoe Drive an impressive arched entrance gate was erected. A road with a thin crust of blacktop was laid in contrived and gentle curves from said entrance gate out to the end of the finger. Two tributaries wandered around the rest of the property. Fifty-six building lots were surveyed and the corners were socked in. Power was run in. Artesian wells hit sulphurous water at a hundred and sixty-two feet, and they were capped, awaiting the houses. John started at the end of the finger, working back.

I drove through the arched entrance and down the winding asphalt. Out at the end of the finger two houses were already up. At the neck of the finger the foundations were sketched in. The houses in between were in various stages of completion on the new raw land. The day was overcast, and sticky as gym socks. From talking to Big Dake, I knew the plans. Two- and three-bedroom houses, CB construction, no two floor plans or exteriors exactly alike. Terazzo floors and cypress and weldwood paneling and pine kitchens and picture windows and window walls and big closets and storage walls and breezeways and terraces and a look of spaciousness. The price, per copy, including the land, of course, would be between thirty-six five to forty-eight thousand. And the construction cost per unit, exclusive of land and fill and dozing, would be such as to give an average profit of twelve thousand per house, which makes a gross of six hundred and seventy-two thousand, from which you must subtract the raw cost of making new land and protecting it with a sea wall.

It was the thing, I knew, that John Long had been preparing for. As I got out of my car and looked around, I could sense how it would be. Lawns and landscaping and sprinklers whirling and kids bicycling up to Horseshoe Drive to check the mailbox, and people sitting on terraces directly over where the trout had browsed through the weeds, where mullet had rippled the bay water, where the skimmers had gone back and forth at dusk, drawing their sharp beak lines on the gray water.

John had a big crew working. Nearly all the building trades were represented. Where the shell of the house was up, electric saws whined and there was hammering. The place smelled of wet cement and burned sawdust and the faint fish-flavor of new land. I went to where they were laying up blocks and asked an old man where Long was. He pointed down to the end houses with his thumb. The Cadillac was parked in the new road. I went down there and I heard his thick-chested voice at a pretty good decibel level. "You are, for God's sake, not framing something by Picasso. You are framing a goddamn doorway so kindly extract digit."

I went in. What, she had said, is wrong with my husband? Nothing, I thought, that a good sharp rap across the nape of the neck with a meat ax wouldn't cure. He stood, his neck bowed, glaring down into the face of an elderly carpenter who stood there with the mild, tired, endless patience of the very old.

"You are framing doors and windows," John said heavily, "and not making jewel boxes, please."

"Sure," the old man said. "Sure."

John Long is five eleven, about an inch shorter than I. He looks as if he weighs a hard-boiled two hundred. He weighs two forty. He carries extra muscle and meat all over him, on jaw, temple, wrists, ankles. He wears his coarse black hair in a brush cut, and there's a lot of gray in it. In repose his face has all the expression of a fractured cinder block. Yet he can turn on an astonishingly boyish and winning smile. Black hair, like wire, coils out of the top of his shirt and is matted thickly on the backs of his hands. He was dressed in khaki, and it was blackened by sweat at the armpits, across the small of his back, around his belt line.

Watching him gave me a few moments of self-evaluation. I had invented the reason for coming out. Now that I was here, it seemed feebler. It didn't have anything to do with Mary Eleanor. I wanted to be noticed. I wanted him to see that Andrew Hale McClintock was still alive, and a shade disgruntled.

He saw me and turned. "Well, what do you want?"

"You're not sore at me, remember? You're sore at him. I just got here." I handed him the estimate and he looked at it. "She phone or something? She in a rush?"

"No. I just thought. I'd bring it out."

"So you brought it out. Now you can take it back and put it on my desk where it belongs."

"I guess I wanted to see how things were coming along out here. Looks like a lot of progress."

"Do your sight-seeing on your own time, McClintock."

He turned his broad back to me and marched solidly toward the unfinished front doorway. I was supposed to leap into my heap and race back to my glass-fronted salt mine. A month before I might have taken it. But, as I have said, I was fed up with doing work that made no real demand on what I considered to be my abilities.

I went out the doorway ten feet behind him, and said sharply, "Hold it, John!"

That brought him up short. He turned around slowly and I walked up to him, just as slowly. "Just who the hell do you think you're talking to, McClintock?" he asked me softly.

"I'm talking, I think, to the guy who pays me. I'm talking to a guy who apparently thinks I'm some stumblebum clerk, or some idiot child. I'm also talking to the guy who painted such a glorious picture of a great and golden future. Sightseeing! You know, I went back after dinner and worked last night. That's something you're not buying with your lousy eighty bucks a week. So let's both admit you've suckered me into doing a year's work for you and paid me off in promises you had no intention of fulfilling. We'll call it quits right now, but we won't shake hands on it."

He stood like iron in a sudden reappearance of the hot sun. In the back of my mind was the uneasy feeling he was going to hammer me one. And in the front of my mind was the thought, Let him just twitch and I'll nail him for luck.

The stillness slowly went out of him; he forked a cigarette out of his shirt pocket with two fingers and popped the match on his thumbnail, never once taking his eyes off mine. His eyes were a curiously pale amber shade, with darker flecks near the pupils. You couldn't see into them. Your look bounced right off.

"Let's get in the shade," he said.

I followed him over and he sat on some cinder blocks in the shade of a wall. His thighs, like chunks of phone pole, looked as if they'd split the faded khaki pants.

"You get pretty hot," he said.

"It's been a long time building up."

"Now you're making a hundred a week."

"If I'm working for you."

He didn't answer that. He looked down the bay toward the distant bridge. It was up, and waiting cars winked in the heat shimmy, and a big cabin cruiser came through.

"Gordy Brogan can handle the men. Big Dake has the construction experience," he said. "Can you handle the two of them?"

"I have to. I kid Gordy along. I ask Big Dake's opinion on things and tell him how smart he is."

"They can't work together."

"That's no secret, John."

"I'll get a girl down in the office," he said. "And I'll get somebody to chase materials." I had the feeling he was talking to himself.

"Then what do I do?"

"Then you'll come out here. Maybe I better fix it so you and Dake and Gordy could finish this thing off."

"What'll you be doing?"

"Yes, I think that might make some sense. And if it has to come out that way, Andy, I'll set it up so there'll be a damn fine bonus for you that nobody can cheat you out of."

"I don't—"

"But you'll have to start out here soon as I can pick up those other people. I'm glad you popped off. I hadn't thought of that. It's an answer." He stood up and hitched at his belt. He looked at me and through me. "By God, when you plan something for as long as I've planned this, you do it, even if you haven't got as much reason as you thought you had."

"Is something bothering you, John?"

He focused on me. "Bothering me? Nothing bothers me long. I was just thinking this wouldn't get finished. Now I know it will, and I can think better."

I said I better get back and he told me he'd locate a girl. I drove back to town slowly. I kept turning over what he had said, like a man hunting crabs around the rocks at low tide. I fitted a lot of kinds of trouble to what he had said, and came up with one answer that fitted everything. Suppose a doctor had told him he was on borrowed time. One of those things that will hit you in six days, six weeks, or six months.

"Even if you haven't got as much reason as you thought you had." No long life to enjoy the money he'd make.

"A bonus that nobody can cheat you out of." After I'm dead.

"And if it has to come out that way." Come out the way the doctor had said.

"Now I know it will, and I can think better." My mind will be more at ease. I can plan things, and see that Mary Eleanor's future is assured.

Truly, I thought, a hell of a thing. A man like that. Tough as mangrove roots. Some little damn thing that muscles couldn't handle. That's the way it went. A man sickly all his life can hit ninety because he takes such good care of himself. It had been almost too simple. I'd turned down Mary Eleanor, and then gone ahead and found out exactly what she wanted to know. And come out of it with a raise. Hell, if he was that sick, I could understand his not wanting to tell her. He'd be smart enough to go to the best doctors and demand the truth. Maybe it wasn't the best policy in the world to keep the little woman in the dark, but it was his business, not mine.

Gordy Brogan called me a few minutes after I was back in the office, sore as hell about some copper tubing he had to have. I told him to hang by his thumbs while I checked. I called Fort Myers and Clearwater and Tampa and found out I could get everything in Tampa. I told them to load it on a truck that wouldn't come down by way of Jacksonville, and called Gordy back and told him when he'd get it, and chided him a bit for not having it on his bill of materials. He blustered and fussed at me, and then calmed down and told me one of his corny Irish jokes and hung up. The sun finally melted the overcast for good instead of popping out for five minutes at a time, as it had out on the job. The hot sun filled the town with live steam. Steve Marinak, John's legal talent, went by and waggled fat fingers at me. He had on one of his notorious shirts. This one was lemon-yellow with big red lobsters all over it. It made me wonder if John had made a will, how long Mary Eleanor would wear black.

I couldn't settle down to the routine work until after I got back from lunch at Saddler's Drugs. At three o'clock a man named Fitch phoned and said that Mr. Long had phoned him and had a girl he could send over right away, or in the morning, whichever was convenient, and he was certain I'd be more than satisfied with her.

Four

I GLANCED THROUGH the big plate-glass window at three-thirty and saw a girl coming diagonally across the street toward the place. From the way she was looking at the sign and resettling her shoulders and pulling her tummy in and walking briskly, I knew at once that this was the item from Fitch. She wore a fawn-colored skirt, sandals, and a white blouse like cake frosting. She had a big red bag slung over her shoulder and she kept a hand on it to keep it from banging her hip. She had brown hair with glints in it, and she was tall and somebody had told her how to walk, and she had remembered and perhaps improved on the original advice. She wasn't carrying much meat on her bones, though giving in no way the slightly scrawny impression of Mary Eleanor. Still, I prefer the proportions of one Christy.

She looked in at me and came through our door and up to the desk, and said, "Are you Mr. McClintock?" When I nodded she gave me a mimeographed form from Mr. Fitch's employment service, with the information filled in, and I asked her to sit down while I studied it.

The voice had put me off a bit. One of those dead, flat Katie Hepburn voices which you acquire because maybe you were sent to Mrs. Potts' Seminary for Young Females, and from there to an Ivy League hunting preserve, and sometimes Daddy would come in the plane and pick you up and you'd shop while he went to board meetings in Manhattan.

I got to the name, which was Joy Kenney. Miss Joy Kenney—and I looked over the top of the paper at her, at arched brows, purposeful mouth, nose wide at the nostrils, sea-gray eyes, and an upper lip just a shade too long.

"You can smoke if you want to."

"Thank you," she said.

The education was public high school and some business college I never heard of. Age—23. Address—89 Taylor Street.

"Live with your folks?" I asked.

"In a furnished room. My parents are dead."

"Brothers and sisters?"

"I have a brother."

"Been in town long?"

"Six months."

"What have you been doing?"

"It tells you on the form, near the end."

"Oh, sorry."

I read some more. Experience—A stenographic job in Tulsa, a secretarial job in Biloxi. And since she had been in our town she'd been a waitress at a restaurant on the north side, one I knew by reputation as being a shade on the greasy-spoon side.

"Funny you didn't stick to secretarial work, Miss Kenney."

"Is it? I couldn't find what I wanted when I came here. I've been listed with Mr. Fitch. He promised that he'd call me when the sort of job I asked for came along."

"What did you ask for?"

"A position where I'd be the only girl in the office, and not a job with a professional man. Real estate, construction, advertising—one of those."

"Why no other girls in the office?"

"Then they're senior to you and they tell you what to do, and I like responsibility, taking orders from men, and being on my own."

I watched the slim hand that lifted the cigarette slowly, too slowly, to her lips—making the gesture self-conscious and contrived. I knew she was trying to look calm. There was a tremor in her fingers, almost too fast and faint to be detected. I couldn't figure it. John Long had undoubtedly set up the wages with Fitch, and I knew they weren't going to be high enough to make anybody tremble. She had the same air about her as somebody putting their last ten bucks on the table and waiting for the dice. As though she had a hell of a lot at stake.

"Why are you so nervous?" I asked.

She shook her head quickly in a way that tossed the brown hair back. "I'm always nervous about a new job. I didn't know it showed."

"Relax, for God's sake."

"I'll try to, Mr. McClintock."

I found a ruled pad and gave her the pad and a pencil. "Here. Just a trial flight, Joy. Letter Henderson and Sons Lumber Company, Twelve-twelve Front Street, Tampa, Florida. Dear Sirs: In inspecting the cypress you shipped us on your shipping order sixteen eighty-nine C, we find that item eight, amounting to three thousand board feet, was not included, even though it appeared on your shipping order."

She was quick and competent. I finished the letter and asked her to transcribe it. She made the old Underwood sound like radio tap dancers, and the letter came out crisp, perfect. I asked her some questions. She knew all the routines of withholding, social security, compensation. She clucked a bit at the condition of the files. She had some bookkeeping. She was willing to go to work right away, so I said O.K. We stood by the file cabinets while I explained the system. Her perfume was faint and pleasantly spiced, and we stood close enough so that I could detect the good clean smell of her hair, see the clean white scalp at the hair roots. It is almost a full-time project for a woman to stay dainty in September in Florida. She was managing.

When I told her she could go to work I was watching her closely, and it was a little like when you tell the butcher he just won the sweepstakes, and he wants to try to take it in stride. I had a hunch her knees were weak.

I phoned Fitch and told him, and then I got her to start calling me Andy. And she asked a few questions about hours, about how to answer the phone. I showed her the equipment ledger, and explained how we had three jobs going, and who was handling each one. We were going over the scheduling of orders when John Long came in at five-fifteen.

"Well," he said, "I see you've got—" And he stopped suddenly as Joy turned from the file cabinet and looked at him. I was watching John's face and I saw something bleak and old and deadly happen to him. It lasted perhaps a full second and his face closed again and he went on, carefully casual, "A girl already."

I wondered exactly what the hell was going on. "This is Miss Joy Kenney, John," I said. "Joy, this is the boss, John Long."

"How do you do, Mr. Long," she said quietly. Her shoulders looked rigid.

"Nice to meet you, Miss Kenney." The air in the office had that pre-thunder feeling, as though a spark would jump off your finger if you reached for a light switch.

John went over to his desk and picked up the estimate, and said, "I phoned her. I'll take this over after I clean up. But I don't think we'll go ahead."

"Won't Gordy be finishing up in about ten days?"

"And I'll bring him and his crew onto Key Estates," he said, heading for the door. I went out with him to the Cadillac. He tossed the estimate in onto the seat. "That girl going to work out?" he asked, too casually.

"She's damn good, as a matter of fact. Did you know her before?"

His eyes looked out of his closed face. "What gave you that ridiculous idea? I never saw her before in my life."

"Sorry. I just had the impression when I introduced you that you had met before."

"I knew someone who looks a lot like her."

"Oh," I said, and watched him drive away.

I went slowly back into the office. Sure, he knew someone who looked like her. And she used to know someone who looked exactly like him. That's why it meant so much to her to land the job. And I was a Lithuanian krull bird, the kind that hangs upside down from pepper trees.

It was most pleasant to have Joy in the office. I sat and tapped my front teeth with a pencil and watched her dredging around in the files. She was working on the bottom drawer, sitting on her heels, and she kept her back straight. I admired the way the narrow waist made a double concave line, like parentheses turned the wrong way—) (—and farther down the parentheses turned the right way ( ), and that, too, was very charming, and as I speculated upon it I heard the sound of my tooth-tapping get slower and slower, so I swiveled my chair around resolutely, wondering what was wrong with me. Good Lord, Andrew Hale McClintock, straighten up. Have you got to go around lusting after every female you see? Keep this up and they'll come after you with nets. Keep this up and you'll start following them on the street, mumbling and leering and wiping your chin on your sleeve. Go fishing, Andrew. Indulge in some fine open-air manly sport and take your little imaginings off this fine new secretary's fine new frame.

At five-thirty, just as I was closing shop, Mary Eleanor phoned.

"Andy? Oh, I'm glad I caught you in. John just showered and went to talk to some woman about a motel."

"I know."

"Andy, you darling, he mentioned that you were out at Key Estates this morning, and I'm so glad you decided to help me."

"Look, Mrs. Long, I didn't—"

"I'm dying to talk to you again, but we're going to the

Beach Club for dinner, and I think I can drive out to see you afterward. It will be late. About midnight, but please wait up for me. Andy, I'm so grateful." The phone clicked. I said hello three times and hung up. I might have been able to break in and cancel the idea, had not Joy been standing waiting to be told to go home.

I offered her a lift and she said no, thanks, she had some errands. She said she was glad to be working here, and I said I was certainly glad to have her here, and we both smiled charming smiles and went our separate ways.

I went to Moger's Wee Supermarket, picked up some groceries, and drove on back, put the stuff away, checked the tide, wind, and daylight, and decided there was enough daylight left to take a fast run out to Horseshoe Pass. I took the spinning outfit, loaded with six pound monofilament, and a plastic box of small plugs. I parked and went out to the end of the sand spit at a half gallop, knowing that daylight, tide, and wind were all conspiring to make some snook unwary. I had the place to myself for a change. There wasn't much left of daylight. I dropped a plug out beyond the riffles and brought it back erratically. A ladyfish took it and I gave her enough slack so she could throw it. Another lady took it and threw it and the third strike was hard and heavy. This snook ran fast and close to the surface and stripped my line off against the drag. It seemed to be going too fast and too far, so I released pressure on the drag. In a strange way, that makes sense. Let up on the pressure and they stop their run. Continue it and they head for Mexico. I tightened up on him again and he ran down the shoreline and took a wide fat jump, splashing hard, and I saw that he was a fine fish indeed. He went deep and pouted, and finally came in, pooped. I got his head on the sand and reached down cautiously and snatched him all the way out of his element and into mine. The mosquitoes were beginning to peel off by squadrons so I hurried on back to the car and drove home. He was just a hair over thirteen pounds. I cleaned him, wrapped him in the freezer paper Christy had given me, tossed his inedible parts in the creek, and carried him down to Christy's. Twenty feet from her place, I could hear her singing. I winced. She couldn't carry a tune in a bait bucket, but it was good to know she'd lost the blues.

I yelled through the screen and went in. I unwrapped him on the kitchen table and he was admired, and she wrapped him up again and found room for him in her two-by-four deep freeze. I built us a drink and we discussed what we'd stuff the fish with, for baking. She was intent on oysters, so I finally agreed to go sloshing out on the flats Sunday morning and get a batch of them, provided she'd make the stuffing. We matched to see whose kitchen we'd mess up right now, and it came out mine, so she told me to go back and fix more drinks and she'd shower and be over with her share of the groceries. She came over wearing more clothes than usual and smelling soapy, with the ends of her hair curled and damp.

"I," she said, "am dressed in this sedate fashion because movies are frigid on the inside, and that's where you are taking me."

I handed her a drink. "That suits me perfectly—on one condition. That we make it the late show and get back here well after midnight."

She sat on the table. "Why?"

"An unwelcome guest is coming. Mrs. John Long."

She stared at me. "Aha! Fatal charm. Serves you right."

"No, look now. Seriously, Christy. It is something of a mess." She listened while I went through the whole thing. How I had gone out there and stumbled right over the information she wanted to know. I went through all my reasoning, including why I wanted to be away when Mary Eleanor arrived.

"Andy, I'm going to borrow your car and go to the movies alone."

"Do you *want* me to get in a jam? Do you *want* me to be here when she gets here?"

"I think it would be terribly, terribly rude not to be here. But there's another thing. I think it's wrong that John Long hasn't told her. I think you ought to tell her."

"That's John Long's business, isn't it?"

"Men are so darn stupid, and they try to be so darn noble, Andy. Any wife wants to know a thing like that. Women are stronger than you men think. It isn't fair of him to deny her the opportunity of helping him shoulder some of the—fear and the worry. So you're going to hint what the trouble is."

"Now, look, I'm not—"

"I'm starving. Fix another drink and let me cook."

Once we were eating, we went at it again, but she was weakening my resolutions. Maybe I would be doing both John and Mary Eleanor a favor to let her know, at least by indirection. I used all my arguments, about how she might go to pieces, how it was none of my business, etc.

"Andy, you just hint around the edges, and if she starts to go to pieces, you be careful."

"You can't hint to a woman and then shut up."

"Oh, just lie, then. That's easy for you, you know."

In despair, I moved over to the subject of Joy Kenney. I covered that topic.

"Hmm," she said, getting up to get us more coffee.

"What's with this *hmm*?"

"Pretty, you said. Very pretty, from that tone of lechery you used, describing her."

"Lechery? Not McClintock."

"Yes, McClintock. And why I should feel at all jealous, I'll never know. Obviously, McClintock, he has been embroiled with that female."

"Embroiled?"

"Think of a better word, and stop inanely repeating mine. A little passing affair. Ha! A typical male indoor sport. And now she has angled her way into the office, and he doesn't dare do anything about it. Or maybe he doesn't want to do anything about it."

"Why do you have to go to the movies? You know all the plots by heart."

She didn't hear me. "Isn't it typical, though. Just what a man would do. Be right on the verge of death, and try to forget his troubles by going out and seducing some helplessly stupid little girl."

"Not helpless, and definitely not stupid."

"Oh, she's smart to let a thing like that happen to her?"

"Christy, you have a great deal of sexual antagonism. Men are just as nice as other people. Nicer, sometimes. You got a sour one once. So are they all sour?"

"Ninety-nine point nine per cent."

"Including McClintock?"

"Including ninety-nine point nine per cent of McClintock."

"Oh, come now, Hallowell!"

She patted my hand. "Don't take it so hard, lamb. Come on. Let's wash the dishes."

She was in a movie mood and she refused to sit around and hold my hand to give me strength until the appearance of Mary Eleanor. At last she wheeled off to the late movie, riding my clutch and racing the motor mercilessly. I took off my shirt, dug out a book, and spread myself on the couch, bug bomb and cigarettes handy. My mind kept wandering off the edge of the page and making tight little circles around Mary Eleanor and Joy. My days seemed to be getting too full of women, all of a sudden. I still didn't know how I'd handle Mary Eleanor's visit. I forced my mind back to the novel and pretty soon I hit a place where the book took over and all I had to do was lie there and move my eyes.

It was eleven-thirty by my watch when the MG came snorting and whuffing down the road and side-slipped into my personal jungle. This time she didn't catch me with the shirt off, just unbuttoned.

She came in as if she lived there, skirt swirling around her lean tan legs. She dropped herself into a chair so hard her legs swung up, and then her heels banged back onto my floor. "God, what a mizrable ole evening, Andy! Just plain terrible."

"You're early. Cigarette?"

"Thanks, dear. I had to get away early or die in my tracks. It was so good of you to change your mind, Andy."

"I want to talk to you about that. Drink?"

"Bourbon, if you have it. On the rocks."

I left her there and went out and made her a fat one. She might well need it. I carried it back in to her, sat down opposite her, and sipped my own drink, smiling like a death mask and wondering how to start.

"Did you find out something, Andy?"

"I want to make it clear, Mary Eleanor, that I made no attempt to find out anything."

"But you did, didn't you? I can tell. You look and act so funny."

"I might have."

"Then you have to tell me. You have to." She had leaned forward, and her eyes looked like black glass.

"I want a couple of things clear. First, I didn't try to find out anything. And second, I don't want the sources to get back."

"You know you can trust me." I heard Christy park my car outside, walk off down the road.

Now I had backed myself all the way into a corner. So I gingerly repeated my conversation with John Long, editing it considerably, and watching her face all the time. She sat utterly still. I wished I had seated her where the light would reach her face. I left some things out, and softened the rest of it.

"Tell me what *you* think," she said, her voice very calm.

"Oh, I think he's a little sick or something. He knows he needs a rest. And he's afraid that will interfere with Key Estates. He couldn't trust Dake or Gordy to do it, alone or together, and—Well, when I went out there, it gave him the idea he could use me along with Dake and Gordy, and get it finished, and it eased his mind."

She took a cigarette out of her evening case and tapped it

sharply on the back of her hand. "The job is going well out there?" she asked.

"Fine, as far as I could tell. Faster than I thought."

"You hinted, Andy, about him saying that one of the reasons, or something, for finishing it wasn't good any more."

"Something like that. I suppose he meant you can't enjoy the money you make so much if your health isn't good. Something like that."

"But he *did* say you wouldn't be cheated out of this bonus you're supposed to get. What does that mean?"

"Well, if he couldn't actively run the business somebody else would have to, and their ideas might be different."

"Did you ask him directly what the trouble was?"

I had expected a rattled woman, and Mrs. District Attorney seemed to have arrived. "I asked him if something was bothering him. He said nothing bothered him long."

"But it all sounded as if he expected—his work to be interrupted."

"That's right."

"And soon?"

"I don't know. He's getting me out there soon to break me in on the job."

"And you think it could be sickness."

"It just—Well, it just sounded that way."

She leaned forward suddenly, her arms crossed, braced down against her knees, head lowered so that I was looking directly at the top of her head.

"It sounds as if he thinks he's going to die," she said softly. "It sounds just like that. Oh, God—"

"It probably isn't that serious," I said.

She sat up, picked up her drink, belted it down without a

pause. As she drained it I heard the shrunken ice cubes clink forward against her teeth.

"What are you going to do?" I asked.

"I truly don't know. If it's something I—something he doesn't want me knowing, then I've got to make out to him like I don't know. I want to thank you for helping me, Andy. It was nice. It was sweet."

"I didn't know it was going to come out this way."

"Of course you didn't. Andy—you won't tell anybody about this? That girl, even."

"No," I lied. "I won't tell anybody."

"He's a proud man. He wouldn't like anybody knowing anything like this."

"Sure."

She got up in a weary way. She said, "How soon will you go out there? To Key Estates?"

"Tomorrow's Friday. I guess about the middle of next week, if he gets a man I can break in on chasing materials soon enough."

I walked her to the door and out to her car. She walked slowly, her head bowed, scuffing her heels. At the car she turned, and said, "If anything—happens to him, Andy, I want you to know I'm glad you're close by."

"Thanks."

She put her hand out and I took it. She held my hand in both of hers. Her hands were small, hot, dry, thin-fingered. There was a feel of restlessness in them.

"I'm still thanking you for finding out, Andy."

Standing that close, with her hands on mine, I became acutely conscious once more of that invisible emanation, that faint tart effluvium of desire. In spite of her spindly little body, the chipmunk look of her face with its dark eyes and oversized front teeth, she had that weird knack of making you overly aware of her femininity, aware of a thin urgency in her body, a sort of prehensile inventiveness. I had the crazy feeling that I could kiss her once, pick her up, and carry her—burning in my arms—right back into the house. Maybe there's an extra sense that enables a woman to sense that particular moment. She let go of my hand and turned and got into her little black bug of a car. I chunked the door shut and she looked up at me. "Anyways, I can see if I can find out what it is. From Dr. Graman. I'll let you know."

"I hope you find out we're wrong."

"I hope so, Andy. I hope so."

Her lights went on and she backed in a sharp arc, shot forward down the road, raining shells and sand into the foliage. She left me feeling ashamed of my base instincts, and impressed by her courage. I pried up the top of my car and rolled up the windows. There was a wind off the bay, driving the mosquitoes inland, and the tide was down so there was a fishy tang in the wind. I wandered down the road. There was a light on at Christy's. I started to look in and then said, "Ooops!"

"Damn Peeping Tom," I heard her say.

I turned my back and pretty soon, she said, "O.K." I turned back and she had a robe on and she was on her stomach on her bed, her head at the foot of the bed, six inches from the screen, the light behind her and showing pale through her hair.

"Don't you ever close blinds?"

"And lose that wonderful breeze? Don't be silly. Out with it, Andy. Did she blow up?"

"She was like ice. I edged up to it. She took it, filled in the blanks. She isn't going to let him know she knows. She's going to check with the doctor."

"That's funny, you know. From what you told me about her before. I thought she'd go up like sky rockets. I was going to trot over when I heard screaming."

"You know, she's attractive in a funny kind of way."

"Oh, dear Lord!"

"It was just a comment. I can make a comment."

"You can make all kinds of comments, McClintock."

I looked through the screen at her. She looked out at me. I heard my voice drop half an octave, as I said, "Here's a comment. You look wonderful. Lovely."

"That's two comments," she said, barely moving her lips. "Keep count."

"I know, I know. And we decided not to—keep on until it was on the same basis as a reflex, didn't we?"

"Shut up. I'm holding my hand. It wants to creep over and unhook the screen."

"I'm always irresponsible after midnight."

"Shut up."

"But you look so damn good."

"Shut up."

"Good night, Christy."

"Good night, Andy."

I walked away slowly, quietly. As I reached the road I heard a small grating click. It could have been the screen hook. I looked back. The window was dark. All of Tickler Terrace was dark, except my empty house. I stood in the night, then wiped the palms of my hands on the sides of my pants and walked toward my place. Partway there I picked up a handful of shells and flung them viciously into the brush. They whipped against the leaves. I felt virtuous, undone, and lonely. I had a noggin twice the size of the one I had fed Mary Eleanor and went to bed.

Five

HAVING, IN MY LONELY SPLENDOR, forgotten to set the alarm, I found Joy Kenney waiting when I arrived breakfastless at nine-fifteen. I let her in and went down to Saddler's and had a quick breakfast.

When I got back Big Dake was waiting for me. His right name is Bigelow Dake, and he looks like something out of the Old Testament. Big, mild, bearded—and full of unshakable convictions about everything. He is a master builder. He was a successful man in Michigan when his wife died several years ago. They were childless, and he decided there was no point in continuing. He sold out, stopped shaving, moved to Florida, built a house with his hands, to die in, then got so bored he had to go to work or go crazy. He has a massive contempt for the short-cut shoddy methods that John Long often uses. If he were willing to accept the responsibilities, he could set up and, with his knowledge, become one of the finest builders on the west coast of Florida, because he has no reluctance about using experimental materials, or building to the most advanced designs. But should he do that, unless he could hire someone to translate his orders to his workmen, he would fail, because there is his weak point, and the one place where he gives me trouble.

He was in, as usual, because of trouble. Half the crew had quit because he had fired one unskilled laborer. I'd fix it up for him to hire the man back and I'd switch him over to Gordy's job, and everybody would be happy. I asked him how things were going otherwise, and he said things were fine, provided you liked your buildings constructed of cardboard and spit, and he lumbered out, looking like a benign bear.

I barely had time to get Joy going on some routine work when Steve Marinak came in, wearing an orchid shirt with gray globs on it. He sat down and panted and thumbed open his briefcase and pulled out an impressive-looking document and handed it to me. "John says for you to tuck this away safe, Andy."

"What is it?"

"Contract between you and John Long, Contractors, Incorporated. He has the authority to commit the corporation. Doesn't make much sense to me, though. The contract does, because I wrote it, but the idea of making out a contract isn't the way he usually operates."

I read it carefully. It was very fine. In the event that John Long, through his own choice, or through circumstances outside his control, was unable to finish Key Estates, I would be placed in charge at a salary of two hundred a week. And as each house was sold at the figure shown in the planning schedule, I would receive a bonus of three hundred dollars. Close to an eight thousand dollar bonus.

It began, almost, to sound as if there *were* opportunities in small organizations. I didn't want Steve worrying about his good friend John Long, so I said, "Oh, I just told John that I'd rather have a contract."

"Is he going to let you finish off his baby?" Steve asked, his round eyes going wide.

"He might. I guess he's got other plans, too."

"Well, come on and we'll get your signature notarized, too, and then you can hide it in some safe place."

We stood on the street afterward and he told me about his two redfish and I told him about the snook, and he said when things were organized we'd have to go out on his boat after some kings. He started away and then turned back, and said, "Where've I seen that girl in your office?"

I named the restaurant.

He poked me with his chubby elbow and winked, and said, "Maybe she can learn to type, too."

"A hell of a reputation I've got around here," I complained. "Fitch sent her over and she's damn good."

"I only wish I had your youthful vigor again, Andrew."

I inferred that he was a disreputable old goat, but he merely looked soulful and plodded away, his red neck on fire in the sunlight. I got back to the office and found that eighteen things were all going wrong at once. The rest of my day was a vague blur of irritation and purposeless energy through which stalked the tall coolness of Joy Kenney, unflaggingly efficient, calm, resourceful.

At the end of the day when I was ready to stagger home, I was perfectly willing to admit that I didn't know how I'd

manage without her. Again she turned down a ride. I col-
lapsed for a time with a tall cold gin drink, then showered
and hunted up Christy.

She told me I looked pretty, and she too wanted to get
away from it all, so we drove up to Sarasota and had dinner
on me in celebration of the raise I had forgotten to tell her
about. We had dinner at the Plaza, compared weather notes
with Randy, and over dinner, I told her about my contract,
which she admired greatly.

"Watch it, boy, or you'll be moving away from Tickler
Terrace. Your position, you know."

"Never. I'm too fond of you common people."

"You flatter us, sire."

After dinner we went over and listened to Charlie for a
time, and we drank out of the cool copper mugs, and maybe
because the piano was saying the right words, or the wrong
ones, we got that feeling of falling into each other's eyes, and
I knew it had been the hook on the screen that had grated,
and I knew it was all something we shouldn't begin again,
that it would do no good, and knew at the same time that we
were going to begin again, because, looking back, we knew it
had been shaping up again for too many long weeks, too
many indeed.

On the way back she sat close to me, and there were Cuban
drums on the car radio, and we had nothing to say to each
other, which, at the time, seemed perfectly right and good.
We were back at one-thirty and my Christy got out of the car
and stretched like a big sleepy golden cat, and we went into
the darkness of my house, hand in hand. In the stillness I
heard a familiar sound that for a moment I could not identify. Then I recognized it as the ping that the back screen

door always makes. I left her and went through the house, just as fast and quietly as I could. I found the switch and turned on the floodlight over the kitchen door. It made a harsh white light on the bushes, and I heard a thrashing and then silence, and a distant pad of feet on the sand road, fading.

She came up beside me. "What is it?"

"Somebody was in the house. I don't know what the hell for."

She laughed, but it wasn't one of her best efforts. "How silly. What have you got worth stealing?"

"It's a point." That made me think of my shiny new contract. I looked in the bureau drawer. It was there.

"Gee," she said, "I'll hate it if we've got to start locking up around here."

"It was probably just an admirer."

"They get pretty eager, huh?"

"Isn't it worth a little risk?"

"Fatuous. That's what you are."

"She works in a bookstore, so now she's got a new word."

We stood still and the night outside seemed a little more alien than usual. As if it had eyes looking out of it. I turned the rest of the lights on and she hugged herself and turned away from me. I could sense her uneasiness.

I went over and kissed her, and in the middle of it she turned away, and said, "But what could they *want*?"

"I told you."

"Be serious, Andy. I don't like it at all."

It's odd how a thing like that can destroy a mood. It put me off a bit, and put her further off. We wandered around each other for a while and then she wanted to go home, and I walked her down there, kissed her sedately on the tip of her

nose, and went back to my place. I have a few—not many—
pet possessions. I started taking inventory. Beside the house
is a thing some madman designed as a garage. I keep everything but the car in there.

It took me about five minutes to spot the empty nail. I felt
forlorn. My Hawaiian rig was gone. My beautiful gimmick
of stainless steel tubing and surgical rubber, complete with
harpoon with swivel barb. Not that I was ever going to use it
again—twice was too much. It took me two water-soaked
hours of flapping around the groins and pilings to get skunked
the first time, and two more hours the second time, complete
with face mask and swim fins, to get close enough to a humble five pound sheepshead which was minding its own business, to pull the trigger when the barb was three inches from
him and run him through. He died instantaneously and I
swam to shore feeling bestial, and knowing that I would do
the rest of my fishing above the water, not under it.

I was never going to use the rig again, but I liked to look
at it, and I liked to see it hanging on my garage wall looking
slim and deadly. Once I had shot it into a palm tree from
thirty feet and it had taken fifteen minutes to cut the barb
out.

At least it solved the prowler question. It was the sort of
thing a kid would steal. But, damn it, I missed it. At least it
started me thinking of fish, so I set the alarm for four-fifteen
and laid out the equipment. When the alarm finally woke me
up, it took me all the way to Horseshoe Pass before I was
completely awake. There was a gray light in the east when I
started. Things were slow at first, and then picked up. For a
time the pass was boiling with big jacks. Some were too big
and I lost plugs. After landing and releasing about ten of

them, I began to get arm-weary and wish for a snook or something I could take back with me. I switched to a spoon, and the jacks kept hitting. I worked the spoon slower and deeper and finally got myself a five pound red. Five minutes later I got his twin sister, and by then it was nearly seven, so I went back across the bridge, rinsed the equipment, cleaned the reds, cut off a slab of one and fried it for breakfast, and put the rest in the refrigerator. By the time I was fed and cleaned up, the world looked like a reasonably acceptable place. There were probably better places, but this one would do.

I went slowly by Christy's but saw no sign of life, so I went on down to the office, arriving at a quarter to nine. The phone was ringing as I unlocked the door, so I strode over and swooped it up. "Good morning. Long, Contractors. McClintock speaking."

A heavy distant droning voice, like a squad of summer bees, said, "McClintock, this is Chief Wargler." I'd never met our police chief, but I'd seen him, and seen his pictures. He looked like his voice sounded, big and vague.

"Good morning, Chief."

"I'm trying to plan out something here. Forgot just— What you say, George? Oh. McClintock, we don't want to do this on the phone and right now I can't spare a man or go myself. Wonder if you'd run over to Long's house and tell his missus he's dead."

"What!"

"Hell, didn't you know about it? I should have thought when that construction fella called in, he'd called you, too. He's out at that there Key Estates of his. First man on the job found him this morning."

"Heart?"

"No, he took his own life, son. It's a little on the messy side. We're waiting on the coroner and then we'll have to get him cleaned up a little before I'd ask his missus to identify him legally. Don't you let her come running on out here. You just find out where she wants the body took, and we'll let her know when it's time to come on down and tell us it was John Long, I know damn well it's John, but we got to do it right."

"Can I come out after I tell her?"

"Why, sure. I see no reason against that. I'll have the boys send the crew home, telling them to come back on Monday, if that's O.K. with you."

"I think that's best."

"Well, you break it to her gentle. She's a little thing."

I hung up. I prayed for a sudden case of amnesia, and I'd have been willing to settle for a pair of broken legs. I guessed he'd started thinking it over, and decided that Big Dake could break me in on the construction end of it. Maybe it had got painful. Cancer or something. So he'd gone out there in the middle of the night and . . . It seemed incredible that he could be dead, all those muscles stilled, that hard body slack. I even toyed with the idea of the phone call being some kind of gag. But nobody has that good a sense of humor this year.

So I drove to their beach house at an average rate of ten miles an hour. I'd never been inside the house before, but I had no interest in the cool look of it, the soft greens and blues, the glass, the low-slung furniture. The maid took me out on the terrace and pointed down the beach to a figure on a dark-red blanket. "She's down there."

I thanked her and walked nine million miles down the beach. The Gulf was a sparkling blue, and the sand was pale cream. A one-legged gull landed and gave me a ruffled, evil look. He was all white, with a black head like a penguin. A line of pelicans went by, wings still, bellies inches from the water, looking straight ahead, and all brooding about prehistory and the dull taste little fishes have had for the last thousand years. And no matter what I did, I was still getting closer to the blanket.

I glanced ahead and saw that I had been wrong about the figure. It wasn't prone, it was supine, and clad only below the waist. I wondered dimly why any woman should want to get her bosom tanned. She had little red plastic cups on her eyes, and she was well greased. I coughed and looked out to sea.

"Why, Andy!" she cried. "No, don't look yet. Now."

She was back into her halter and sitting up. "What is it, dear?" she asked. "You look awful guilty."

"Well—" I started. I was doing fine. Writing a truly great script for myself. "Well—it's John. There's been . . ." I stopped. I was damned if I was going to say there'd been an accident. It's one of those situations where anything you say sounds as if they'd start selling soap just after you finished. I dropped to my knees on the corner of her blanket, sat back on my heels, and took her hand. In spite of the sun, her fingers were frosty.

She looked at me with a child's soberness in her eyes. "He's dead," she said in a small voice.

"Yes."

She pulled her hand away and stood up. "I've got to go to him. Where is he?"

"They don't want you to go to him. It's not—very pleas-

ant. They want to know where you want him taken. You can
see him there."

"Taken?" She looked dazed. "Oh, I see what you mean.
Yes, he has to be taken somewhere, doesn't he? Dangerfield's,
I guess. On Jacaranda Street. It's next to—But they'll know,
won't they? And I've been here in the sun—telling myself
that everything would be . . ." She went down on the blanket like a doll tossed onto a bed. She fell awkwardly and cried
awkwardly, and I patted her greasy shoulder and took my
hand back and wiped it on the blanket, while she moaned,
"Oh, oh, oh, oh."

Women have many kinds of tears. There's a kind they use
on you, a contrived and delicate weapon that leaves them
looking pretty. And there's a healthy, lusty, snorting,
boohooing brand that leaves them reddened, puffy, moist,
happy, and beautifully relaxed. In that case it seems to be a
form of self-therapy. Then there are the tears of agony,
which must feel like acid. The gray and twisted tears, when
they don't know or care how they look. When you can walk
them back to the house, as I walked Mary Eleanor back, and
they stumble and lean on you and don't know who you are,
or care. I led her inside and made her lie down, and I dark-
ened the room and sat near her until Dr. Graman could ar-
rive. She rolled her head from side to side, and her thin fingers
kneaded her flat brown belly, and not knowing, you could
have thought she was in acute physical pain.

Graman came quickly. He gave me a distant, sour, who-
are-you-sir look, and assembled a sterile hypo. He was real
pretty. He looked a lot like Rita Hayworth wearing a false
mustache. He had heard about John Long five minutes before
I called, and I had caught him as he was leaving his home to

come to see Mary Eleanor. He led me to understand that he could handle things, that she would go to sleep, that he would have a nurse come over, and I could depart.

I wasted no time driving from the house down to Key Estates. A police car was parked just inside the entrance and a uniformed young man with his thumbs in his belt stood astride the road until I had identified myself. A hundred yards down the drive I passed John's Cadillac. I went out onto the end of the finger and parked near several other cars, one of which was a police sedan, and another I recognized as belonging to Jack Ryer, local newscaster, local columnist, local wire-service correspondent, local intermittent legman for the Ledger when fat stories broke, local man about town, and—according to my sources—competent local collector of female scalps, though not of the bundle-and-brag school. I have bent elbows with him and he is a most pleasant drinking, poker, and fishing companion, though many consider his charm to be applied with a shade too clumsy a spatula, and there are those who say that he laughs with a very cold eye indeed. He is what is called clean cut and well set up, and they say he is not long for our town, as he has that integrated manner of a national phenomenon.

He came around the corner of the house nearest completion, and he was wearing his abnormally alert look, yet under the look was a grayness like the cinder blocks. He stood and lit a cigarette and had to move the match a half inch to the left to get it close enough to the cigarette. He looked at me and then said, "Yo, Andy."

"Where is he?"

"Other side of the house." Jack sat down on a cinder block and licked his lips and studied the toes of his shoes.

The ambulance came crawling down the new blacktop behind me. I went around the corner of the house. Chief
Wargler looked at me, and said, "You're McClintock. Tell
her, did you?"

"And called a doctor. He's to go to Dangerfield's."

"I figured so." He was wide and he blocked out what the
coroner was bending over. Other men stood around with
that particularly useless and thoughtful expression worn in
the sight of sudden and violent death.

I moved around Wargler. John lay on his back, his head
braced at an oddly nauseating angle against a lumber pile.
One leg was outstretched and the other leg was doubled up,
the knee canted outward. Beside him was one shoe, the sock
laid across it. A pale gray sock with a chinese-red clock. He
wore a white shirt and gray slacks. There was a great deal of
blood. He looked smaller, and older, and grayer, and
shrunken. From the throat socket, at an angle, protruded the
gleaming stainless-steel haft of the sort of harpoon they use
in skin fishing. His right foot was bare. Near the coiled fingers of his right hand lay a Hawaiian rig. I saw the scratch in
the metal where I had banged it on a rock. I saw everything
clearly. Every pebble and tiny fragment of white sun-hot
shell, and every splinter on the edges of the boards in the
wood pile. His face was turned so that the eyes, dry of mois-
ture, seemed to look at the haft of the slim harpoon. There is
seldom expression on the faces of the dead. Or perhaps, there
is only one expression, always. A look of austere, remote,
and yet humble dignity. As though they say, "All along I
knew I was clay. Now see me and know thyself."

The white shirt was unbuttoned and peeled back from the
left shoulder. The coroner reached down and pulled the ther-

mometer from the armpit. He looked at it and looked at his watch. He was a small man with a look of eternal indignation.

"With the goddamn sun," he muttered to himself, "and the heat, who can tell a goddamn thing? Sometime between midnight and five-thirty, or maybe even six."

I looked at my rig and I nibbled the tip of my tongue. What to do? Point and say, "Hey, that's mine!"

Maybe you do. Maybe there are a lot of people in the world who go around instinctively doing the logical, uncompromising thing. Maybe they haven't any imagination, too. I'm always blundering around paying so much attention to what other people could think, that I'm always balanced on a rough rail of indecision, tarred and feathered with my own doubts.

I lit a cigarette and it tasted like burned farina. I found out that there are two ways of gagging. One is in the throat—a very ugly spasm. The other one is back in the mind, and you wish it were in your throat.

The coroner fussed and muttered and wrote things down. Two frail clerical men brought the basket woven of metal straps. They set it down, argued about the harpoon and what to do until the coroner, in a fury of impatience, wedged the heavy body over onto its side, grasped the bloodied barb, and pulled the haft quickly and neatly through the torn wound.

Wargler said, in his buzzing voice, "By Henry, when I get around one of these days to killing myself, I'd sooner stick this here muzzle in my mouth than pig-stick myself with that darn thing. George, Marvin got all his pitchers. You set that wicked thing in the back of the sedan. You there. Take that shoe and sock along. George, you and—you there,

McClintock, give those puny fellas a lift on that now they got him strapped in. John was hefty."

We grunted up with it and slid it in. Wargler came over and said to the driver, "He goes to Dangerfield's, and you there, you tell Billy Dangerfield to make John look perty enough real quick so his missus can come identify."

Six

EVEN BEFORE I GOT BACK to the office, it was becoming apparent to me that the firm of John Long, Contractors, Inc., was in a fine mess. It would have been all O.K., and if not O.K., at least a hell of a lot better, if John Long had been less secretive about his business affairs. At no time had I been given any overall picture of what was going on. I had my routine chunk. Steve Marinak had a portion. Another law firm, and a firm of accountants in Tampa, had some more. And apparently Harvey Constanto of the Gulf Savings and Trust knew a little more. But no one of us had enough of the jigsaw pieces to make the whole puzzle.

All I knew was that there was a lot of stuff on order, a lot of stuff on hand, a fat payroll to meet, and a dingy little bank balance with which to meet it. Whenever the operating balance had begun to get low, John would make a deposit from another account. If Key Estates was going to continue, somebody would have to fatten the kitty. I hoped that somebody, somewhere, would find a report from John describing exactly how he operated.

I parked near the office. I could see Joy Kenney in there typing away. I could see a woman waiting to see me. I sat in the car for a few minutes, wondering how it was to hold that barbed razor against your throat and release the friction trigger with your bare toe. Would you shut your eyes? It was sickening. Maybe he had wanted to talk to me. Waited around, wandered around the place, found my rig and took it off the nail, and then decided there wasn't anything to say, after all. And I'd come back with Christy, and he had gone out the back and hurried away. Then, perhaps, he'd gone out to take a look at the big dream, take a look at Key Estates, which had been going to turn him into a rich man.

I could sense that the whole town was buzzing with it. I could see people standing in shop doorways, looking over at me and at the office. I went on into the office. Joy glanced up at me and murmured good morning and I knew at once that she knew. Her face was waxy. She looked through those eyes at me, and I felt as if the eyes were both long tunnels, and she was crouched 'way back in there, looking through the tunnels, hiding back there where nobody could find out what she thought or felt.

The one who was waiting was the lady who wanted to build the motel. Happy Saturday morning. She was wound up tight. No salutation. No weather comments. "Young man, all day yesterday I thought about the rudeness of Mr.

Long and the way he turned me down after promising to build for me, and I wish you to inform him that I have seen my attorney and if he knows what is good for him, he will go ahead with what he promised to do. I am not accustomed to being spoken to in the manner in which he spoke to me, and furthermore, I—" She stopped and stared at me, aware that I was trying to say something. "What is it? Has he reconsidered?"

"He's dead."

She stared at me some more and then sat down a bit bonelessly. "Oh, dear. He was such a *nice* man. An accident?"

"He—uh—committed suicide sometime very early this morning."

"Oh, dear. Dreadful. Dreadful!" She got up and fooled with the clasp of her handbag and made a vague about-face, and headed toward the door. "Oh, dear," she said again, and the screen door hissed and closed after her.

Joy looked at me across the top of the typewriter. "The girl from the dress shop came over and told me."

"Little round girl?"

"Yes."

"That's Nate. Natalia. She's a Russian."

"Oh."

"I went out there."

"I thought maybe you did."

"I can't quite—take it all in. As though any minute he'll walk in. A very lusty alive guy."

"He—he seemed to be."

"I guess he was sick."

"I couldn't understand what he did it with."

"One of those things they use to shoot fish underwater."

"Like a gun?"

"More like one of those crossbows, only without the bow part. Surgical rubber instead. In the—uh—throat."

"He—did it to himself, then?" she asked. Her mouth worked soundlessly.

"I can't see somebody walking up and doing it to him, if that's what you mean. He had his shoe and sock off so he could work the trigger with his toe."

Looking at her as I explained it, I could have sworn that I saw a lot of tension go out of her. She half closed her eyes and seemed to sway a little. I got up quickly and went to her. "You all right?"

She gave me an almost formal smile. "Yes. Thank you." I went back and sat down.

The door was yanked open and Gordy Brogan came steaming in. He came over and put his hands flat on my desk and looked down at me. He is an Irishman, professional variety. Peat bog, potato famine, when Irish eyes are smiling in a whisky tenor, smoky whisky and all. As he is at least fourth generation, he has had to develop his own brogue. It isn't genuine, but it gives the impression.

"By God, Andy, this is hell!" he said. He was too upset to remember the brogue.

"It's rough. Sit down."

He sat, his blue eyes intensely serious, for once. "What's going to happen?"

"You guess."

"Man, I'm done out there in a little over a week. Where was I going?"

"He was going to haul you over to Key Estates."

"And now?"

"Stop asking me. I don't know. The operating funds will run for maybe three weeks."

"Why does a man go and do a thing like that to himself, I'm asking you?" The brogue had begun to reappear.

"You do it when you have reasons, they tell me."

"And his little lady? And how is she bearing up?"

"Not good."

"Aaa, the poor little thing. It's alone she is now." He suddenly became aware of the sound of a typewriter and looked over at Joy. "Say, I was wondering what lovely girl voice it was answering the phone when I called."

"Miss Kenney, Mr. Brogan," I said.

"It is an improvement, indeed," he said, beaming. And then he apparently remembered John Long again, and his face became lugubrious. "The best I can do, lad, is go back out and finish my job, I see."

"That makes sense. They were paying on the basis of percentage of completion, but they weren't paying into our operating account. The last quarter payment is due as soon as they inspect and accept."

"We'll carry on for John, God rest his soul." He went out and climbed into the pickup truck and rattled back toward his job.

I hadn't the slightest idea of what to do. Close the office—Was that what you were supposed to do? I wanted somebody around to tell me what to do. My executive talent had a few mothholes in it. Disuse, perhaps.

I got up, and said, "Hold the fort, Joy. We'll close up at noon. I'll be back. If anybody wants me, I'll be at Mr. Marinak's office."

"Shall I call and make sure he's in?"

I went to the door and looked diagonally across the street and up at the second-story office. I saw the wild flare of a shirt through the window. "He's in."

I went over and up the stairs, and Steve's gaunt girl told me I could go on in.

Steve gave me a quick glance and said, a bit too heartily, "Set, Andy."

"You know about it, of course."

"I know about it. What's on your mind?"

"I want to know what happens now."

"In what way?"

"With the business. The operating funds are a little feeble. But it is a corporation, I understand. Who makes the decisions now?"

"We don't know. Not until we get an order to open his lock box over at Gulf Savings and see if there's a will in there. He held the controlling interest. Mary Eleanor owns about thirty per cent of the outstanding shares. I've got a few. Harvey Constanto has a few."

"You don't know if there's a will?"

"He never made one out with me. That isn't saying there isn't one. He never let anybody know all his business. If he died intestate, the court will appoint an executor, probably Gulf Savings. Mary Eleanor will have the controlling interest. Until it's settled up, the executor will be able to release funds from other accounts to keep the business rolling. We'll have a sort of a directors' meeting once we find out how the shares are split up."

"What would you suggest I do, Steve?"

"Carry on. What else? And you have got that contract you—asked for."

"Actually, Steve, I didn't ask for it. He insisted."

I could detect a faint unpleasant aroma of unfriendliness. "That isn't what you told me, Andy."

"I know. I'm sorry about that. Poor judgment."

"You're sitting pretty."

"I don't just know as I care much for your tone."

"Suit yourself."

We stared at each other and then he smiled apologetically. "Hell, I'm sorry. I'm just damn upset, that's all. I want to kick something. You were handy. Truce?"

"Sure. I know what you mean. I'm ready to bite, too."

"I tried to get hold of Mary Eleanor. Some woman told me she's sleeping."

"That's the nurse, I guess. Graman gave her a shot."

"She that bad?"

"I was there. She's real bad."

"That's damn funny," he said, talking half to himself. "They haven't been getting along worth a—" He caught himself, looked embarrassed.

"I thought they were getting along fine," I said.

"Skip it."

"Sure, Steve."

"I'll let you know when I know something."

"Thanks."

I went down the stairs and back out into the sun heat. Wilburt's Book Nook is three blocks up the main drag. I decided to walk, and wished I hadn't, because about seven people stopped me and asked about it. I said the same things over and over, and they listened and licked their lips and looked like the people who always stand in the street to watch somebody jump off a building.

Christy was on a small ladder rearranging things on a high shelf, and Wilburt was leaning with his elbows on the counter, his eyes a bit glassy, trying to take sneaky looks at her legs. The scene gave the impression that nothing up on that shelf had needed rearranging.

He jumped a bit, and said, "Greetings, Andrew. Kindly accept my sincere regrets on the demise of your employer."

"Thanks, Will." Christy turned and looked down at me, her eyes concerned.

I said, "Can I take that big lush blonde out for coffee?"

"Please do," Will said.

We walked up to Saddler's and picked up coffee at the counter and carried it back to a shiny blue booth. Christy said, "It's a terrible thing."

"It is. Go ahead."

"Go ahead what?"

"Aren't you going to ask for a lurid description?"

"Dear, please don't snarl at me. I know all I want to know, thanks."

"Sorry, You're a happy exception. I should know better."

"I'm sorry, too. You can snarl if you want to. I can guess how you feel."

I lowered my voice. "Not entirely, you can't."

"What do you mean?"

"That rig he used—mine. After I walked you back last night, I took an inventory of the garage. That was the only thing missing."

She raised her hand slowly to her throat. Her wine-vinegar eyes went wide, like a startled cocker spaniel. "Oh, my goodness!"

"At least that. And oh, my gracious, too. So it was old John pounding off into the shrubbery."

Trust women to be very much to the point when somebody tosses blue chips on the table. "You told them it was yours?" she asked.

"Didn't seem to be the time or place."

"You bought it in town, didn't you?"

"Yes, from Wally Farmer. At the Tackle Shop."

"Won't it be—Well, sort of routine to check and see where it came from? Like they do with guns?"

"They might. I don't know."

"It happened early this morning, didn't it?"

"Yes. Why?"

She looked down into her coffee and blushed bright pink. "I couldn't sleep. Nerves or something. I walked over about five-thirty. You were gone and the car was gone, so I guessed you'd gone fishing."

"I did. Got a couple of reds. Didn't you hear me come back in?"

"No. I took a pill and went back to bed. Did you go fishing with anybody?"

"No, I didn't."

"Who was out there? Did you go to the Pass?"

"Not a soul. I had it to myself."

"Andy, I think you took me fishing with you."

"What the hell are you talking about?"

"Andy, if they find out that thing is yours, and that you were out on the key at the same time he's supposed to have done it . . . I mean it's all silly, but people always try to make something out of a suicide. You know that. And I bet people have seen you with that Mary Eleanor. I just think I went fishing with you and . . ." She looked up quickly beyond me and smiled, and said, "Hi, Jack."

Jack Ryer came to the booth, gingerly carrying a full glass of Coke. He put it on the yellow composition table-top, and said to Christy, "Hi. Shove over, kitten. Give Uncle Jack room."

She shoved over and he sat down, glanced at his watch. "Jeez, what a morning, kids. I got the newspaper stuff written, and the program set up for the twelve o'clock news, and I feel eighty-five years old."

"You may be tired, but don't lean on my girl," I said.

"He's light as feathers," Christy said. "Aren't you, dear?"

"Feathers. Off horses. Andy, what the hell?"

"Those are my sentiments," I said. "Suicide always seems like a very unpleasant sneer at the rest of the human race."

"Suicide. Wargler jumped at that. It's a hot September. You know how it goes. If a masked man shot the teller over at Gulf Savings, Wargler'd consider suicide first."

"It's plain enough, isn't it?"

"Because his shoe and sock were off? Because his prints will no doubt be on that gizmo, if Wargler ever thinks to have them brought out? Is it too hot for you too, Andy? Use that little pointed head."

"Tell me how."

He leaned forward, his eyes intent. He wagged a finger at me. "O.K. I'll tell you how. Psychologically it stinks. People cutting their own throats are rare as great auks, much less harpooning themselves. That's what got me going on it. So,

when I get going, I do research. I did some research at the
Tackle Shop right after I got back Wally had one left. Same
model. John Long had a pair of arms on him. Hell, they practically hung down to his knees. I bet he had four inches reach
on me. And I can hold one of those things against my throat,
with harpoon or whatever you call it all loaded in there, and
push the trigger with my thumb. So somebody shoots him
and takes off his shoe and sock and Wargler is happy. At least
he'll stay happy until I can talk facts of life to him. Some of
the facts being that a well-off, healthy guy like John Long
just doesn't knock himself off, and if he does, all he has to do
is take one of his own pistols. John had about four hand guns,
and I know because I've seen them in his study, with nice
little boxes of shells right next to them in the bottom desk
drawer."

"Maybe he wanted to use two hands to steady the thing,"
I said.

"Your pointy head is showing again. John could have
steadied a railway gun with one of those hands of his."

"Maybe he wasn't healthy."

"He certainly wasn't puny."

"A bad heart doesn't show. Cancer doesn't show at first."

"Oh, come off it, Andy. Face the facts of life." He looked
at his watch again, drained his Coke, and got up hastily. "Got
to run check the teletypes, kids. Thanks for the Coke." Six
feet from the booth he turned, and said, "You might catch
the program today, children. I'm going to give the good
Chief a hotfoot."

"See what I mean?" Christy said softly, after he was far
enough away.

"But everything fits the—the other!" I said.

"Does it? Does it now? Think back, Andy. Think hard. Maybe he *knew* somebody was going to try to kill him, and he was afraid they'd make it. Wouldn't that fit just as good as the sickness theory? I mean, the way Mary Eleanor said he was acting at home. And trying to make provisions for the future, and all?"

"Hold it a minute. Look. You got to know something about John Long. Not too long ago a guy sitting in a truck gave John some lip. John reached in through the window and grabbed the front of his shirt and yanked him out through the cab window and heaved him up on top of his own load of gravel. If he thought somebody was going to kill him, he'd go find the guy and beat hell out of him."

"What if he didn't know who it was? What if there were—oh, unsuccessful attempts?"

"Would he go wandering around alone at dawn, then?"

"If he thought he could grab the person trying to do it. But the other person was quicker."

"And the other person picked out my place to come to and steal the weapon?"

She looked at me with an intentness I had never seen on her face before. "Yes, Andy. *If* that person were very, very clever. If it is accepted as suicide, they are all right. If it is accepted as murder, then who can be made to fit? Andy, I went fishing with you this morning—if that isn't enough—I spent the night with you."

She was being my girl. My eyes felt funny. "Look, I—"

"Andy, you're too trusting. Please."

"They'll take you for a ride in the paper."

"I've been for a ride in the paper. And it almost could have been true, you know. It almost was true—last night."

"Look, you're making me nervous. You're scaring me."

"I think you'd better be scared."

"Will that be a healthy condition?"

"The best. Then you won't be silly. I've got to get back so Wilburt can put me back up on that ladder."

"Catch Jack's program."

"I wouldn't miss it for the world."

I went back to the office and fiddled around there for ten minutes, then went out and turned on the car radio. His program was sponsored by Gulf Savings. I hunched in the seat and rattled my fingernails on the horn ring and wondered what he was going to use as a hotfoot.

Seven

JACK COVERED INTERNATIONAL and national news first, and then I could hear his voice change as he got to the local news. You could almost hear him smack his chops.

"John Long, prominent building contractor of this city, was discovered by workmen this morning, dead on his development on Horseshoe Key which is called Key Estates. He had been shot through the throat with a barbed harpoon propelled by an underwater fishing device activated by heavy rubber bands. Chief Wargler investigated in person, and came to the *immediate* decision that it was suicide, because the dead man's shoe and sock had been removed from his right foot.

"We have made it our practice to report the news. Today we plan to editorialize a little. We want to ask Chief Robert Wargler certain questions. The deceased could have pressed the trigger mechanism with his finger—why was the shoe and sock removed? Could it have been to mislead you into thinking it was suicide, Chief Wargler? Why is no attempt being made to trace the sales of such devices in this area, to determine if the deceased owned one? Why did a man with a drawerful of guns select such an unusual device? Why was there no suicide note? Why was the sock right side out? Wouldn't a man intent on suicide rip off his sock in a hurry and leave it wrong side out? Why was the victim's car left so far from the scene of death? Could he have been meeting someone? Could he have been merely inspecting his property? Chief Wargler, could this not only have been murder, but also rather clumsy murder? Why, if your supposition is correct, did the deceased sit on the ground, when it would have been handier for him to sit on the lumber pile nearby? These are the questions to be answered, Chief Wargler."

The station announcer came on with his commercial and I turned off the set. Jack Ryer was a very persuasive guy. Hearing it over the air somehow made his case sound a lot stronger. It gave me a cool feeling at the nape of my neck. Joy came over to the car and asked if it was all right to leave. I told her to go ahead. I locked up, and drove to the police station. It is a building constructed during the boom of the twenties. It looks like a Moorish house of ill repute. Some dark gluck which once coated the roof has melted and run down the sides of the building. Just as I reached the front steps, Wargler came out with the Cro-Magnon type called George. They both looked as if they had just shut their fingers in a door.

Wargler looked at me, and asked, "Something on your mind, son?"

"I just listened to Jack Ryer."

It wasn't the best opening gambit in the world. George looked speculatively at my stomach and seemed inclined to lift his right foot off the steps.

"Durn amateurs monkeying around," the chief said.

"Well, I heard what he said about checking whether John owned one of those Hawaiian rigs. I don't know whether he did or not, but the one that he used was mine."

I stood there trying to look burnished and bright and clean. Two sets of hard little eyes studied me. Wargler took a kitchen match out of his shirt pocket and put it in the corner of his mouth.

"Now what do you know about that! You hear that, George! How'd you find out it was yours, son?"

"I knew it as soon as I saw it. It has scratches on it. I recognized those."

"Now we didn't hear you say it was yours."

"I guess I was in a state of shock," I said.

"If it's yours, McClintock, what in the wide world was John Long doing with it? He borrow it or something?"

"Well, you see, mine was stolen last night. At least I think it was stolen last night. I mean, I hadn't really looked at it for a couple of weeks, I guess. But last night I noticed it was missing."

"After dark you noticed it was missing?"

"Yes. You see, I kept it hanging on a nail in my garage. So after I took—took a girl home, I came back and looked around to see what was missing."

"You think she'd stole something?"

"No, dammit, I just—"

"Don't you cuss me out there, son. You just answer the question I put to you."

"Look, I came over voluntarily to tell you about this."

"But it was *after* you heard that son-of-a-bitch on the radio, wasn't it? We got to keep that in mind, don't we? And now I'm asking questions. Did you think that girl stole something. And who was she?"

"She's Christine Hallowell and she works at Wilburt's, and I don't think she'd steal anything anytime. I came back with her and I heard my back screen door and I ran through the house and turned the floodlight on in back and I heard somebody running off. That's why, after I took her home—she lives almost next door—I checked to see if anything was gone. And that thing John used on himself was gone."

"So, like a good citizen ought to do, you quick phoned up the police and we came out and investigated."

"You know I didn't do that."

"But I don't know *why* you didn't. Ought to phone in when you hear a prowler."

"I haven't got a phone."

"You got a car. I know because I can see it right there."

"It was pretty late and I was tired."

"How late?"

"Sometime between one-thirty and two. I thought it was some kid. And by that time he was long gone."

"How did he bust in?"

"Nothing is ever locked out there. Nobody locks anything up. The garage doors were open."

"Why did you look out there?"

"I told you. To see what he took. I was checking on all my stuff."

"And you looked to see if that spear thing was took, and it was?"

"It was gone, I told you. But I can't be sure it was taken last night. It could have been—"

"Getting pretty gad durn upset, aren't you, son?"

"Chief, I came over because I thought you ought to know about this. And I think that's doing my duty as a citizen."

Their eyes were like little stones. I heard a vast belly rumble, but I couldn't tell whose it was. They were no longer looking as though the end of the world was just over the hill. They looked speculative, and faintly smug.

"But you didn't say anything this morning out there, McClintock, and now you come running and a-bleating when you hear it come over the radio. Well, we're going to check on who has those things around here. Isn't that right, George?"

George nodded solemnly.

Wargler went on, "George, you go pick me up sandwiches. Two liverwurst on rye with lettuce, no mayonnaise, and a chocolate shake. Take time to eat for yourself. But don't take too long because I'm about to faint of hunger. You come on in, McClintock."

We went to his office. On his desk there were framed photographs of pistol meets and a picture of a defeated-looking woman with two adolescent, equally defeated-looking daughters.

He had me sit down and he puffed around, wheeling a gadget over, plugging in a hand mike. He said, "Now this here is one of our new methods, and by God you do it right, hear. I'll ask the question and hand it over to you and you give the answer in it and hand it back, and while you're talking in it, keep this little black thing shoved down with your thumb."

"O.K."

He started the visible tape going, and said, into the mike, in an officious voice, "Subject: Interrogation of suspect in Long murder by Chief of Police Robert A. Wargler."

"Now wait a minute!" I said.

"Shut up," he said. He stared at the mike. "Oh, hell! That went on the tape. Now I got to erase that."

"Don't call me a suspect, damn it!" I said.

"I told you you don't get no place cussing me, son. And what the hell do I call you?"

"Call me a person who volunteered information."

"That make you feel any better?"

"A lot better."

"I'm not saying you're not going to be a suspect."

"When I am, I won't talk without a lawyer. And if you call me a suspect on there, I won't answer your questions."

He started over again and got the date and time. "Now, your full name."

I gave that and my address and my place and date of birth, my present employment. The yellowish tape rolled from one reel onto the other and we handed the mike back and forth solemnly. He got onto the theft, and it was just about the same as it had been out on the steps—only more so. Where had I been with Christy? Did I know her well? How long? George came in about then with the food, so the chief shut off the machine, patted it and ate with dogged concentration. George sat and stared at me. I once had a friend with a well-trained Doberman. He'd lie all evening with his muzzle on his paws and hang that same unwinking stare on me and keep it there, until by the end of the evening I was pretty jumpy.

"Where were you early this morning?" Wargler asked.

"I went fishing."

"How early?"

"Before five."

"You didn't get to bed until after two and you got up before five? That sounds kind of funny to me."

"I like fishing."

"Where'd you go?"

"Horseshoe Pass."

"That's about two miles from that Key Estates, isn't it?"

"That's right."

"Catch anything?"

"Two reds, about five pounds apiece."

"What'd you get 'em on?"

"A number two Drone, working it slow and deep."

"You alone out there?"

I thought of the look of worry and fear in Christy's eyes. I'd made one mistake. A lie was going to be another mistake, I was certain. "Completely alone. In fact, I didn't see a soul."

"You didn't go take a look at Key Estates, did you?"

"No."

"Didn't happen to kind of run into John Long?"

"No. I didn't see anybody."

He took the mike back and sat with his lips pursed for a time, then pressed the button down, and said, "Conclusion of first interrogation of McClintock."

"First interrogation?"

"We'll think of a couple more things to ask, son. This whole thing sounds mighty funny to me. Don't you think so, George? Son, who do you think took that thing out of your garage?"

"I thought at first it might have been John. Then he ran off because he decided he didn't want to talk to me after all. But the more I think about that, the less I like it. I guess what Jack Ryer said started me thinking."

"Thinking about what?"

"It makes more sense, thinking of what kind of man he was, to think that somebody killed him. I guess taking that thing of mine would make it look as if I did it. At least, it would be a sort of red herring."

"What else you got you want to tell us?"

There were quite a few things in my mind: Mary Eleanor's request; the new contract; the odd scene between John and Joy; the way John had talked to me out at Key Estates. I had a sudden realization of the way they'd look at me if I tried to tell them that Mary Eleanor had asked me to find out what was wrong with John.

"That's all. I just thought you ought to know about the rig and that it was stolen from me."

Wargler stood up. He seemed to be trying to remember something. His face cleared as he remembered his lines. "You stay in town, son, hear?"

"I'm not going any place."

It was an effort to keep from sidling furtively out the door. Once I got back out to the car I felt better. It would have saved a lot of trouble and a lot of tension if I'd been able to give the same information while I stood beside John Long's body. But, after a crumby start, I had recouped my losses, and felt better. And it hadn't been necessary to lie about Christy. I didn't figure that would have done either of us any good.

When I got out to my place, Big Dake was waiting for me, sitting on my front steps and smoking his pipe. We talked it all over. He had some thoughtful things to say about how in the midst of life we are in death, and so on. I could see that he was deeply and profoundly moved, but he had an irritating way of sounding like one of the earlier prophets.

"I wonder what will happen to Key Estates," he said.

"You bring up an embarrassing point, Dake."

"Do I?"

"I have a contract to take it over. Oh, I don't mean buy it. I couldn't buy ten shore feet of it. I mean to be in charge of completion."

"Great God!" he said wonderingly.

"I know. What will they think of next? You know and I know that I can't do it without you. You wouldn't be working for me, except nominally. From a practical point of view, it will be the other way around, I guess. I need your opinion on this. We could combine the whole three crews and make Gordy Brogan a kind of labor foreman. Then you can keep on the move, telling Gordy how things have to be done. And I can run around yipping, and do the paperwork, and chase materials."

"I don't believe Brogan will take my advice, Andy."

"Hell, I can kid him into it."

He thought it over, tapped out his pipe on my steps, and stood up. "It might just work, Andy. I'll do some thinking on it tonight. You say you have a contract? I've been with him a long time, and we've never had a contract."

"I think he thought something was going to happen."

"You don't think he killed himself, then?"

"No, Dake, I don't. I did—but now I don't."

"That's a terrible thing, to take a life. God gives life. The person who takes it has to be a devil."

"I guess so."

He pulled at his beard, lifted his big broad chest in a sigh, and got into his car. He waved once as he drove away slowly. Before I was in the house, a police sedan drove up, bringing Wargler, George, and a young cop I hadn't seen before. It turned out his name was Jimmy, and he carried a fingerprint outfit.

They dusted my back door handle, and the interior knobs, and looked sagely at the two reds and looked at my spinning outfit, and stood in my garage and stared at the empty nail. Jimmy took some flash pictures here and there, seemingly at random. They went away talking in low voices among themselves.

I was suddenly aware, simultaneously, of hunger and weariness. I ate a couple of fast sandwiches, drank a full quart of milk, stripped down to my shorts, and went to sleep on top of the sheets—went to sleep like falling on a horse that was galloping too fast and too far.

When Elly Tickler woke me by screaming through the window, I saw that the sun was down pretty far. I sat on the edge of the bed, everything blurred and out of focus, and she yelled again, "She's hanging on."

"What? Who?"

"She's on my phone. Some woman. How do I know who? Next time, Andy, I'm coming with a bucket of ice water, I swear. Now get a move on you."

I took a few seconds to splash cold water in my face. Then I pulled on my pants, stuffed my feet into moccasins, and went out to where Elly waited impatiently.

Eight

I TOOK LONG STRIDES down toward Elly's place at the entrance, and she padded along beside me. It took unusual circumstances to betray Elly into that much effort.

"Heavens, isn't it awful! On the radio and in this evening's paper. Now there was a man."

"Sure was."

"A man with a lot of juice. A real man–type man like my Sam was. Once we didn't have a jack and Sam held up the front end of the car while Terry changed the tire."

"Uh-huh."

"Who do you think gigged him, Andy? A real crime of passion, I'll say. With a woman in it someplace. God, you got a long pair of legs on you. You watch. A woman, and I'll betcha bottle of rye."

"No bet."

"Then you know! Come on, Andy. Tell old Elly."

I went on in and back to the phone on the hall table and picked it up. "This is Andy McClintock."

The voice was lost, and far, far away, as it said, "Andy. This is Mary Eleanor."

"Oh. How are you feeling?"

"Far away from myself. Like I was two people. Oh, Andy, it's so dreadful. Could you come over?"

"I guess so. You sure you want to see me?"

"Of course I do. Or I wouldn't ask you, would I, now?" Coquetry seemed automatic, artificial, like a smile painted on a mask. "I sent that nurse on home, and the doctor phoned me and I told him I slept fine and I guess I'll be all right. As all right as I *can* be." There was a little dry click in her voice. A ghost sob.

"Half an hour, then."

I hung up and Elly was leaning over me. "You *saw* him, didn't you? With that thing in his neck. Dear God, it must have been grim."

"Now, Elly. You behave."

"I saw that big fat Wargler driving in and out of here. What'd he want?"

"Don't tell anybody. I'm a suspect."

"You! They *must* be hard up."

"Elly, I got a date."

"Can't you talk to me at all?"

"Tomorrow. I'll talk tomorrow."

"That's a promise now. A true promise. I'll be around."

I went back to my place and took a fast shower, put on a dark blue short-sleeved shirt and oyster-colored slacks, and pasted my hair down with water. I drove out to their house—

her house. The black MG was alone in the curved drive. The maid let me in the front door and pointed a spectral finger toward the terrace. I went out. The sun's rim was almost touching the flat gray-blue of the gulf. She wore a flouncy yellow skirt and a narrow black halter, and she sat tipped back in a barwa chair, looking at me through the V of her bare feet, an Old-Fashioned glass cradled in her hands, the way a child holds a mug.

Her face looked stained, tear-battered, and slightly drunk. She held up her glass. "Here. And one for you."

The trick rubber bowl of ice and the bottle were on a narrow table against the terrace wall. I fixed and took hers to her, sat down on the wall with mine.

"I guess I'm pretty terrible, sitting like this and drinking and wearing such a real loud bright skirt."

"Not so terrible."

"It only happened this morning. But it's like it was weeks and weeks ago. Like he'd been dead—See, I can say it—like he'd been dead for just *so* long."

"That's the shot he gave you. It will do that. That's why they give them."

"I'm glad you came, Andy. I don't want to drink all by myself, and keep wondering why they want to come talk to me in the morning."

"Who wants to come talk to you?"

"That big fat silly old Chief of Police we got here. What does he want with me?"

"He's got it in his head that it was murder."

She had the glass halfway to her lips; she stopped it in midflight. I couldn't read the odd expression in her eyes. She was silent for what seemed a long time. Then she drank deeply, lowered the glass, and said, "Poo. He's just trying to make a real thing out of that job of his."

"Jack Ryer thinks it was murder, too."

She flared right up over that. "Who cares what he thinks? He thinks he's too damn good for us."

"And I think it was murder, too, Mary Eleanor. And by now, I'd guess nine-tenths of the town thinks so."

"I hate this terrible dusty little old town and I'm getting out of it, too. I'm going away just as soon as I can. And stay away. You'll see."

The sun was all gone and there were no clouds to make a sunset. Just a vague red glow way out there at the horizon, with the blues and grays moving in on us. Something chased bait a hundred feet from shore, and they flashed in panic, like new silver dollars thrown flat and hard so that they skipped.

"He'll ask you, Mary Eleanor, where you two went last night, and so on."

"How do I know where John went? We'd go out together when we had to, when there were people and places where we had to be together. Other times I never knew, and I gave up telling him where I was going."

The maid came out, and said, "O.K. I'm going now, m'am?"

"Goo'night, Ephaylia."

"You be all right, m'am?"

"I'll be all right."

The maid gave me an obscure and opaque glance, and left. Mary Eleanor held her glass out with childish imperiousness. I fixed her drink and took it back to her and sat again on the wall. I was puzzled.

"Mary Eleanor, you made it sound as if you and John were very close until he started acting—odd. Now you make it sound as if you weren't getting along."

"Don't think too much, Andy. That's what gets people in trouble. How much can I trust you, Andy?"

"If you hadn't already decided to, you wouldn't ask that."

"You're too smart about me, honey, I think."

"Get to it, Mary Eleanor. Why did you call me over here?"

"Don't be cross with me. Please, dear. I looked all over the house, Andy. All over. It's something I lost. I won't tell you what it is. Maybe John took it. Maybe he took it and put it in his desk down at the office. Go look in his desk down there, Andy, honey, and find it for me."

"Oh, great! Find something when I don't know what to look for."

"Oh, it's a brown envelope. So big." She made the size of an eight-by-eleven envelope with her hands. "Addressed to me. Mailed from Miami some time ago. It's addressed to me so you know it's mine, and I want it."

"You want me to go snuffling again. Is that it?"

"Just for me. For Mary Eleanor. Sad widow girl."

"No. I got into this somehow and I am now detaching myself as carefully as possible, and I am not going into his desk for even a yellow pencil."

"You look in there and find it and bring it to me."

"No."

"I'll give you—five hundred dollars. You go right now and look and here's his keys." She threw them at me. I caught them. It suddenly occurred to me that maybe I could make a good impression on Wargler by turning them over to him. I tossed them on the table with a mental note.

"Bring it to me when you find it, and don't peek."

She was beyond reason. I wondered how much she had managed to soak up since awakening. The husky belts she had taken since I'd been there hadn't done her much good. The empty glass rolled out of her hand and broke on the terrace floor and she giggled. She swung her legs out of the barwa chair and stood up, took two wobbling rubber-legged steps and lurched at me and clung, saying softly, "Oooo, Andy. Old Andy going round and round. Sit still."

"You better go to bed."

"Take me to bed, old Andy. Carry. Never make it with everything all tippy."

I picked her up—a very light-weight package. She clung to me and called out the turns. There was just enough light in the house so I could avoid the furniture. I took her in and put her down on the bed. She'd laced her thin fingers together at the nape of my neck and she wouldn't let go of me.

"Lie down, old Andy, and hold me tight."

It is an odd kind of irritation and embarrassment, like getting your foot stuck in a wastebasket. She had a wiry strength in those thin arms. She meeched onto me, and was nibbling wet little kisses along my jaw line. I reached back and got her hands untangled and pushed them back toward her and she swung a leg over my arm. As I was getting that unhooked, she latched onto my head again. It was like walking into too many cobwebs in the woods. She was breathing like a little furnace, and smelling like old Kentucky mash. I finally got all of me loose at once and went back like a guard pulling out of the line when the ball is snapped.

"All right for you," she said. "All right for you!"

"Yes, indeed."

"Don't you dare go now. You come right here."

As I went through the house I heard her yelling at me. I stopped and went back to the terrace and picked up the desk keys and went on out to the car and drove away from there, breathing a little hard myself, but not from any unrequited desire. More like the guy who, with a hop, skip, and jump, slams the cage door a half-step ahead of the panther. It was about seven-thirty. As I drove I tried to make excuses for her. Liquor plus loss plus emotional turmoil equals ... That didn't work, and I couldn't even figure myself as virtuous, because I hadn't denied myself anything I wanted. And I knew that if Andrew Hale McClintock had succumbed, it would be the kind of memory I couldn't scrub off my soul with a wire brush.

As I drove through town I started thinking about the envelope, and about my personal involvement, and the hard little eyes of George and the Chief, and about how Mary Eleanor had led me to believe she and John got along fine, and Steve refuting that little misdirection. No, I wasn't going to search his desk, but I made myself a fat excuse to go to the office. Some details about Key Estates to check. And who had a better right to be in the office? That ambitious intelligent young McClintock guy, of course. I parked and whistled cheerfully as I crossed the sidewalk to the door. I unlocked it and went in, and gave John's desk a sidelong look as I went to my own. The lamp on my desk left John's desk in semidarkness. I wondered if, perhaps, there was a completion schedule for Key Estates in John's desk. If I was going to run the job, I would have to know about that. Of course. And so I went over and selected a desk key out of the batch of keys she'd tossed at me.

The key went into the shallow middle drawer of his desk. Unlocking that would unlock both tiers of side drawers. The key went in easily, but it turned too freely—turned with a little grating sound of broken parts. I turned on his desk light and examined the lock. The wood was gouged where it had been pried, and the latch had snapped off. It took me ten minutes to go through the desk and find there was no schedule on Key Estates—and no brown envelope. There was nothing personal in the desk—just forms and drawings, and magazines.

I closed his desk up, turned off the light and went back to my own desk. I sat on the corner of my desk, rubbing my chin, trying to be logical. My desk lamp was canted just enough so that it gleamed faintly against the big front expanse of glass. I saw a tallish man standing there, looking in. It gave me a jolt. And a most odd impression. An impression that is hard to describe. It relates back to something I hadn't remembered in years.

I was one of the scrubs and they had us scrimmaging against the varsity offensive team. I was a linebacker. Their fullback kept barreling in on fast-breaking plays. I was getting intensely weary of the whole thing. He went all out, every time, and when he ran over me, I'd pick myself up from under him, and say stuff like, "How about an autograph?" and "Does this go in the record books?" Quaint, like. But he'd just look at me. Just look. And it was like talking to a fire hydrant. I began to think this was a real eerie guy, though hitherto he had showed signs of modest intelligence. There was something even a little spine-chilling in the way he looked at me.

Scrimmage ended, and what did he do but walk right into

the shower in full uniform. They led him out and fed him smelling salts and slapped his face and he just looked at them. Then they took him to the infirmary and diagnosed concussion, and later he couldn't remember anything that had happened all afternoon after the second play when he apparently had shoved his head against somebody's knee.

And that was the sudden and unpleasant impression I got from just a few seconds' glance at that face outside the window. A mindless automaton, a sort of ritualistic thing, like a machine hiding behind a face. And he went away. Another set of bells was ringing in my mind, but I couldn't catch the tune. There was something else I was on the very edge of knowing, or realizing, and I couldn't figure out what it was. Somebody walked over my grave, and with the shudder came a duck-bump collection. A tall man somewhere in his twenties, perhaps, giving an impression of pallor and vague shabbiness, and something less than human. You just didn't want to be out in the night with one of those loose.

So I was almost happy to see George and Chief Wargler as they waddled through the doorway.

"What are you doing in here, McClintock?"

"I work here, Chief."

"During the day you work here. What you doing in here at night time?"

"I work at night, too, sometimes."

"Where have you been since you left Elly's place?"

"Mrs. Long phoned and wanted me to come see her. So I went to see her."

Wargler hovered close to me. "Been drinking, haven't you?"

"Yes, sir."

"Pretty chummy with Mrs. Long, I figure."

"You don't figure very good, Chief."

"I can figure a lot of things. You think you've been pretty damn shrewd, son."

"Now just a minute. I—"

"We had us a busy afternoon. Talking to a lot of people. Finding out a lot of things, by God. And you're coming along right now. We got a cell for you."

"What kind of gag is this?"

"No gag, son. Come on. You lock up your car and it'll be all right here."

"I want to call a lawyer."

"You got anybody in mind, special?"

"Well—Steve Marinak."

Chief Wargler snickered in a singularly unpleasant way. "Phone him. He happens to be at his house now."

I looked up the number and phoned. Steve answered.

"Steve, this is Andy. Our Chief of Police has some startling ideas and I need some legal talent before he gets carried away."

His voice, in answer, was hard and tight. "I wouldn't bring you a bucket of water if you were on fire, you son-of-a-bitch." He made my ear ring, he hung up so fast.

"Didn't want the case, did he?"

"Apparently not." I tried to think of someone else I could call, and then I suddenly decided to skip the whole idea. Let Wargler lock me up and make a damn fool of himself. Steve's reaction had distressed me more than I was willing to admit. He had been damn near a friend. "O.K., Chief. No lawyer, then. On second thought, I don't need one."

Wargler snickered again. They drove me in, and the two of them filled the front seat completely. We got back to his office, this time with the lights on, and he fiddled with his tape toy some more. This time I was a suspect. And he headed it off with a question about whether I was aware that anything I might say could be held against me. I took the mike and said that I was, and he said it might take some time, so I better move around next to him so it would make the routine with the mike simpler. He explained there was one on order which could pick up a voice from anywhere in the room, but it hadn't come yet, though he expected it any time now.

We sat chummily side by side. "Now, McClintock, did you drive up to Tampa and stay there over the night of August twenty-third?"

I stared at him. "I guess the date is about right. Sure. I was chasing some electrical fixtures. Why?"

"Do you deny that you met Mrs. John Long there for—uh—immoral purposes?"

"I certainly do, for God's sake! What are you—"

"Now settle down, son. I'm doing the asking. Do you deny that on last Wednesday night you went to a bar with Mrs. John Long and you left together?"

"No. I did that, all right, but—"

"Did Mrs. John Long come to your place of residence very late on Thursday night, day before yesterday?"

"Yes, but—"

"You plain stop putting those 'but's in there, son. In a town this size people get a pretty good idea of what's going on when you start stuff like you been doing. Now I had a stakeout down the beach, and I got a report on you from tonight. By God, the same damn day you killed John, I got a witness to you holding his wife in your arms, and if I couldn't get in trouble for doing it, I'd purely beat the hell out of you, old and fat as I am."

I think I tried to smile. I don't think it looked so good. Maybe more like a leer. Those little pebble eyes looked at me with righteous disgust.

"If you'll give me a chance, Chief, I'll explain it. I know it looks bad—I can't help that—but I can explain."

He laid a paper on the desk. "Ever see this before?"

I picked it up. "Sure. It's a contract. How did you get it?"

"Took it out of your place, son. All legal, with a warrant. And it's evidence. Know what it shows? By God, it shows motive. And we got Steve's statement that you asked John for it, and Steve told us it's mighty unusual for John to have fooled around with contracts. He was all upset and he was scrapping with his woman, and he suspicioned somebody messing with her, but he didn't know yet it was you, and you figured you had to fix him before he fixed you, you knowing what a temper he had."

"Are you asking questions, Chief, or making up fairy tales?"

"You go on like that and I surely will slap the hell out of you. Where were you early this morning?"

"That's on the other tape. You've got a complete schedule."

"Want to change any of it?"

"Not a damn word of it."

"When did you really get those two reds, son?"

"Early this morning. Just after first light."

"Now I'm going to turn this off and let you listen to another tape we made this afternoon and then we'll get back to the questions again."

The way they were both looking at me made me feel very uneasy. The gadget didn't have a very good sound reproducer. It had a thin metallic quality. But Wargler leaned back and folded his fingers over his paunch and cocked his head on one side, and we heard the familiar voice say, "Christine Hallowell."

"Now wait," I said.

"Shut up and listen, damn it."

". . . did you come to see me, Miss Hallowell?"

"It's about Andy—Andrew McClintock, Chief Wargler."

"What about him?"

(Wargler muttered, "Too damn close to the mike.")

"Well, you see, he told me about how Mr. Long was shot with his gun and spear, and I—Well, I thought it might look bad for him, and I thought he'd try to protect me or something."

"Protect you from what, Miss?"

"This isn't easy to say. We went out together Friday night. To Sarasota. We got back late—and then he heard that prowler. We've been pretty close and—The idea of a prowler sort of scared me, so I just stayed with him. I—I didn't go home at all."

I had my hands gripped so tightly my knuckles ached. A condescendingly lecherous note crept into the Chief's voice. "You do that often."

Her answer was barely audible. "Quite often."

"Then you went fishing with him?"

"Oh, yes."

"He catch anything?"

"Two reds. About five pounds each."

"You like fishing, Miss?"

"Oh, yes. But I'm not very good at it."

"You know tackle and all that?"

"Yes. We've fished quite a bit, Andy and I." I could smell the trap coming. I wanted to reach out and put my hand over her mouth. Wargler was wearing a sleepy, satisfied smile. And my respect for him upped a notch.

"What did McClintock get those reds on?"

She knew what I usually used. I hoped she'd say she hadn't noticed. "A small buck-tail dude."

"Where were you while he was fishing?"

"Oh, right near him."

"Did you see the fella in the boat out in the pass?"

"I—I might have. I can't quite remember. I guess there was a boat."

"Funny thing. That fella saw McClintock, but he didn't see you."

"I—I don't know how that could happen."

"You know the penalty for perjuring yourself, Miss?"

"I—What do you mean?"

"You didn't go fishing with him, now, did you?"

There was quite a long pause. Her voice suddenly eager, said, "All right, I didn't. I lied because I want to keep Andy out of trouble. But if that man in the boat saw him, that's just as good as if I were there, isn't it?"

"There wasn't any man in any boat, Miss."

"Oh—Oh, dear!"

"McClintock sent you in, didn't he?"

"No, he didn't!" She was indignant.

"He could get you to do about anything he wanted you to, couldn't he?"

"I guess he could, but this was my idea."

"You sure he wasn't coaching you when the two of you had your heads together in Saddler's this morning?"

"No, and I don't care what you say, he couldn't do a thing like that."

"But you got so worried you come in here and lie to us like this?"

"You got me all confused now."

"How long you been sleeping with McClintock?"

"I haven't got anything more to say."

"We could lock you up right now for perjuring yourself."

"Then go right ahead."

"You know about his affair with Mrs. John Long?"

"He hasn't had any affair with Mrs. Long."

"That'll be all, Miss. We'll be calling you in again."

Wargler turned off the machine. He removed the tape, handling it carefully. He winked at me. "That one didn't work so good for you, son. Nice hunk of woman. What bill of goods you sell her? I wished I knew how you slick articles make out so good. Wouldn't you like to know, too, George? Now empty out your pockets, son, and give me that belt and those shoelaces, and we'll just put the stuff right here in this envelope and seal it."

They took me out in the hall. There was quite a crowd. George and the Chief hustled me along, my toes barely touching the floor. A flashbulb went off. That was the picture they printed on the front page of the *Ledger,* me looking like a slack-jawed, guilt-crazed cretin. "LUST KILLER TRAPPED" the headline said. The picture hit newspapers all over the country via wire service. My weapon, my motive, my opportunity. They don't need much more. But they didn't release it until the next morning when Mary Eleanor became the stained heroine by confessing how I had brutally blackmailed her into further dalliance through threat of exposure.

Nine

THE NOISE FROM THE DRUNK TANK woke me Sunday morning. I wasn't among the common people. I had a little hidey hole of my own, with bunk, sink, toilet, and one metal chair bolted to the floor. I had neatly arranged my pants and shirt on the chair, laceless shoes aligned underneath. Some people in the drunk tank were being wretchedly ill, and my stomach coiled sympathetically.

I washed, dried my hands and face on the corner of a sheet, and yearned for my toothbrush. My window was covered with heavy steel mesh in a diamond pattern. I was on the top floor and from the window I could look down the sleepy slant of the main drag. The morning sun was beginning to stream in, and I had the unhappy realization that by noon the cell would be like a Dutch oven.

I couldn't shed the idea that it was all farce, a big fat monstrous joke, and they would let me out, everybody laughing.

About an hour later the jailer, a subdued little wooden-legged man, allowed as how he could go out and buy me a breakfast, and if I signed the slip, he could get the money from the Chief, the money that had come out of my pants.

He brought me breakfast and I sat on the bunk and ate it. I made up the bunk. I counted the diamonds in the window mesh. I made faces out of where the water paint had flaked off the walls. I counted the lace holes in my shoes. They'd left me my watch. I took my pulse. I stared out at the main street. I made hand shadows in the sunshine—cats and swans and a nobby face chewing. I remembered and relived my first date, redrove my first car, tried a mental game of chess and got stuck on the third move. I decided I was not the jail type, and it would take me about two full days to go crazy.

It was a little after ten and the cell was getting hotter and hotter when the jailer let Jack Ryer in. I found out that when you are in a cell there's no good way to greet a visitor. If you sit and sulk you are melodramatic. If you leap up with a grin, you are full of false cheer.

"Relax, for God's sake," Jack said. He tossed the magazines and the carton of cigarettes on the bunk. I took the clothes off the chair and he sat down.

"How do I look?" I asked.

"Legally, you stink. You ought to hear them. They knew all the time there was something evil and creepy about you."

"That's nice."

"I went through that phase, too."

"I would dearly like to bust you right in the mouth, Jack."

"You do, and I won't leave the magazines. I said 'through' that stage. Remember?"

"Where are you now, then?"

He propped his ankle on his knee. "Wargler gave it to me, step by step, proud as hell. Played his tapes. By God, you come out an unsympathetic character on those tapes. Snotty. And Christy, the silly fool, she helped a lot."

"The motive was good."

"And the performance was unspeakable. Anyway, I've now decided, no matter how good you looked for a while, that you are not the pigeon."

"Gee, thanks."

"Just on this basis. I'm always aware of people. Always watching and thinking and figuring. And, my friend, I come to the semireluctant conclusion that you are just not that stupid. I'm not talking about your ability or lack of ability to kill anybody. In that I am not interested. I merely say that if and when you do, it will be a much more workman-like job. Of course, I *do* have one more point which, to me, is damn near enough to clear you, but it isn't legal evidence."

"What's that?"

"I was privileged to listen to some amateur dramatics this morning. Mary Eleanor applied the clincher. She tearfully told me how you forced your bestial attentions on her, and she is just a little bitty girl, and she submitted to your animal violence. And thereafter you bent her to your will saying you would expose the vile relationship should she strike out for freedom."

I stared at him. "The hell you say!"

"Oh, yes, indeed. Mary El is fast on her feet when she senses that she might get wound up in something unpleasant. And it was a quick fast way out of a spot where it might look as if she aided and abetted in the demise of hubby. But that routine of hers cleared you in my mind."

"How?"

"I think that everything that wears pants and travels even close to Mary Eleanor's group has been aware for lo these many years that she is—Shall we say, eminently and startlingly available. Maybe you and John were the only two guys in town who didn't know that. She is, ah, classic word, insatiable, irritating, and not cautious enough for my taste, in addition to being constructed a bit like a wire coat hanger. The male contingent, wary of John's muscles, has contributed most of the element of caution. I confess that I was enticed some time back. I quit with a mixture of self-disgust and terror. When did you start with her?"

"I didn't."

"What? I heard the tape. You admitted you were taking her out, and that she came to your place. What else in the wide world could have been on your dim little minds? Political science? Canasta?"

"She came to me and asked me to help her. She wanted to have somebody find out what was wrong with John. She said he was moody, silent, and even weepy. So, damn it, I had a weird conversation with John last Thursday morning, and he talked as if he wasn't going to be around long. I thought maybe he was sick. So I reported that to Mary Eleanor. It seemed to upset her, but not as much as I thought it would. Now it looks as if he thought he wouldn't be around long because somebody was going to kill him and he knew it. No passes were exchanged until yesterday, and then she made a pass that was a real dilly. My God, I felt like the baby that picked up the fly paper."

"Unfortunately, I know what you mean. I didn't have your moral courage."

"So John knew somebody was going to kill him, and where the hell does that leave me? That's why he had the contract made out. So he'd be sure of somebody being willing and eager to finish Key Estates according to his plan, rather than having the whole thing sold to somebody who'd do something different with it."

"Who can you sell that to? Besides me, I mean."

"Christy knows just how it was. She had a play by play as it was happening."

"Damn it, Andy, it doesn't make enough sense. John knew somebody was going to kill him, so he went out there and made it easy. And the mysterious somebody goes and takes your gun thing to do it with."

"Maybe they would have taken anything handy. Anything you could kill with. A gig or fish knife or gaff."

"True."

"With a feeble attempt to make it look like suicide."

"If you're selling that, friend, you are not going to run into many buyers. You've got to have more—a lot more. And a lawyer. Hell, I'll bend the public's ear a little, but they are going to be in no mood to listen to me."

"You heard the tapes. What was that Tampa thing on August something or other?"

"The twenty-third. Mary Eleanor told them you forced her to meet you up there."

"I didn't see her at all."

"They found out from the maid she was away overnight, and they checked with Brogan and found you were away overnight the same night. Can you give me something to go on? Give me some way I can prove you didn't meet her up there?"

"I didn't know I was going to have to stay over. I hadn't made any reservations, and I couldn't get a room at the Tampa Terrace. It was so damn hot that I thought I'd better get where it would be cooler, so I drove out the causeway to Clearwater, about twenty miles. Let's see, now. I had a couple of drinks and dinner at the Belmonte after I registered in at a Clearwater Beach court called, let me see—Blue Vista Courts. That was it. Right on the Gulf. They'll have the register card. I bought a toothbrush and a razor. In the morning I drove back to Tampa, made my calls, and drove back here."

"Could you have smuggled a girl into your room?"

"Without any trouble, I'm afraid."

"But Mary Eleanor has no way of knowing you stayed in Clearwater?"

"No way at all. I mentioned it to Christy. She'd have no reason to tell anybody. It isn't what you'd call an earth-shaking hunk of information."

He was silent for a few moments. "Well, that gives me two things to work on. One, to show that she couldn't have been with you. Two, to find out where the hell she did go, and who she met."

"Because whoever she met might have killed John."

"Why? Having him around never exactly slowed her up."

"I don't know. It's a hunch. Money, maybe."

"Money from who? And why?"

"Marry Mary Eleanor right now, and you'd marry a nice thing."

"She won't marry anybody. She did once, and it cramped her style."

"O.K., so I'm not making sense."

"Anything else I could work on?"

"Work on Steve Marinak. I could use him. I'm sore at him, but that doesn't make any difference. He's a good trial lawyer, they tell me."

"He is that. Right now he thinks you're a fiend."

"Then if you can make anything out of that Clearwater angle, use it to prove to him that she lied. And if she'd lie about that, maybe he'll figure she lied about the rest."

"O.K. I'll try it." He stood up.

"Why are you going to bat, Jack?"

He smiled. "Not for you, ducky. For the news values involved. I just want to keep this story running. It ends too quick if they elect you." He went to the door and whooped for the jailer. He turned, and said, "Any other little thing?"

I thought of the envelope and the fractured lock. I said, "I'd like to see Christy. Think you can work that?"

"It might be rough. Can try, though."

"Thanks. And thanks for bringing the stuff."

I heard him walk down the corridor, heard him laugh at something the jailer said. The long sticky-hot hours went by. I read everything in the magazines, even the ads. The jailer brought me a tired lunch bought with my money. Somebody had a radio going—hillbilly hymns. Traffic moved on the main drag as though it had been drugged. Some damn kid kept ringing a bicycle bell for no apparent reason. A stupid fly kept sitting on me.

It was two-thirty when the jailer got me and led me downstairs to a small office. It had windows like mine and contained a table and six chairs. Christy sat at one of the chairs, her shoulders hunched, frowning as she dragged on a cigarette. She stood up quickly as I came in.

The jailer said, "Fifteen minutes," and closed the door and

left us alone in there. It was just a little too neat and too co-operative.

I held Christy in my arms and she started crying, saying, "Oh, God, Andy. I messed everything up. I messed everything up."

"Honey, I can only hold onto you with one arm, because they took my belt and I have to hold my pants up."

She started to giggle through the tears and it had a thin little hysterical sound in it. I said, "Whoa, baby. You did what you thought was best. I'm not mad." And I put my lips close to her ear, and said, "I hope you have a pencil and paper."

She caught on, went to her purse, and opened it. She had an address book and one of those pint-sized ballpoint pens. I took them, and said heartily, "Well, tell me how things are."

She began to prattle on about how Elly felt and how Ardy Fowler felt and how they and nearly everybody else out there were pulling for me and saying it was all some kind of a dirty frame-up. I showed her what I had written. It said, "M.E.L. gave me keys, requested I search J.L.'s desk for brown 8 by 11 envelope stolen from her, addressed to her. Desk lock broken. Don't know who."

She nodded, and I said, "Well, it's nice to know somebody is pulling for me."

I motioned to her to keep talking, which she did. And I wrote, "Outside door O.K. Maybe new girl. Remember something funny there?" She was talking and reading over my shoulder and she squeezed my shoulder to indicate she understood what I meant.

"Snuggle up to her," I wrote. "Pry around."

I looked up at her and she nodded as she kept on talking. I tore the page out of her book and ate it. That faint hint of coldness in Jack Ryer had made me decide that it would be a lot better to trust Christy with this new factor.

I kissed her and she clung and said she was sorry all over again and I told her to hush up, and finally got her smiling. Tentatively, but at least smiling. A nice big bundle of girl. Big and brown and warm. Her eyes were a little puffy, but she looked good in her white skirt and green blouse, so I kissed her again, and the man knocked on the door and came in.

"Got to take you back," he said.

She asked me if I needed anything, and I said I better have something to read, and she said she could fix that. I watched her swing down the hall toward the stairs, and then I went back up to my hotbox.

Some fat historical novels arrived an hour later. Ten minutes after they arrived I was in the middle of a hot sword fight and the heroine was lashed to a gun carriage, and her dress was torn just enough, like on the dust jacket of the book, so that you could see her truly awe-inspiring breasts. And, aye, she was a torrid, hot-blooded wench, a fit companion for my dark, thrilling handsomeness.

I was slowly but surely driving Baron Von Schteygel toward the ship's rail when Wargler came in and plumped himself down on my chair, curled his finger along his forehead, and snapped sweat onto my cell floor.

"What were you looking for in John's desk, son?" he asked.

"Why don't you go get your tapes and do it right?"

"Ran out of tapes. But there'll be more coming."

"I accept your apology. Do you think I broke his desk open?"

"Who else?"

"Go look in that envelope full of my junk. One batch of keys isn't mine. They're John Long's. I busted open the desk because I was too lazy to find the right key. Now go away, pretty please."

"Where'd you get his keys?"

"I tore them from the little pink helpless hand of a sobbing woman."

When I looked up from the book again he was still there. After a while he went away. I didn't miss him a bit. Five minutes later the Baron was in the drink and the triangular fins of the merciless demons of the deep were cutting toward him.

Ten

MY FIRST VISITOR Monday morning came at ten. It was Steve Marinak. He wore what was, for him, a subdued shirt. A little candy-striped number in seersucker. His red face was creased with lines of fatigue and embarrassment.

I was well into my second historical novel. This heroine was even more astonishing in a mammiferous sense. I tossed it aside and didn't get up. The cell door closed behind him. He trudged over and glared down at me.

"All right. All right. Do you want a lawyer?"

"I haven't made up my mind yet, Steve."

"I'll make it up for you. You want a lawyer."

"Maybe I do, and maybe I don't want you."

"I don't blame you. O.K., I was a damn fool. I'm supposed to believe in the laws of evidence. So I run with the pack, yelping for your blood. Remember, John was one of my best friends."

"I sort of liked him myself." I linked my hands behind my head and smiled blandly up at him.

"Can I be your lawyer?"

"Please?"

"O.K. Please."

I stuck my hand up and he took it, almost shyly. He said, "Good. Some things you do, you don't get a chance to settle the account. This time I get a chance."

"What changed your mind?"

"A chat with Ryer. Hell of a chat. At first you could have heard us as far south as Placida. Finally I stopped yelling and started listening. Then I talked to Mary Eleanor on the phone. You stayed with her in some little old hotel in Tampa and she was too upset to remember how you registered or the name of it, even. And then I phoned the Blue Vista Courts and they read the name on the register for the twenty-third, including the license number of your car. That made the first hole. Jack's logic widened it: That boy should have been a lawyer." Steve sat down.

"What do we do now?"

"You tell me every last damn thing you know about this whole thing. Everything. Every bit."

"Maybe I'd rather stay here. Maybe I'm getting a nice rest."

He jumped up. "Stop grinning like a damn idiot. Don't you know these people are all ready to crucify you? Get it in your head that this is serious. The prosecuting attorney has been over the evidence. He's about ready to approve a first-degree charge. He's a shrewd guy and it seems to satisfy him, and there isn't much time, because once these things get set up for trial, it's damn hard to make anybody back water."

"Relax. Sit down. I'll tell you the whole thing."

It took a long time. He asked questions, interrupting me from time to time. They were pertinent questions. He made me go over conversations. I gave him every last little detail. Then he got up and paced around. He slapped the wall with his palm and paced around some more.

"Here's one angle. We've got to offer an alternative. We can make her look bad, catching her up in that lie. We can make everything slant as though he was afraid she was going to kill him, to get her freedom. That would be something he couldn't fight. And we can show that she had a chance to find out you don't lock your house, find that thing hanging in the garage. We can show that she wrapped you all up, and practically put an apple in your mouth. And Ryer told me enough—and I already knew enough anyhow—so we can show her up for the nasty little nympho she is."

"Only one flaw in that. I can't quite believe it."

"Why not? The more I think of it, the better I like it. She came to you with a phony investigation she wanted you to perform. I tell you we've got to get them off on some other scent, some other possibility, good or bad, to get you out of here."

"I still don't want an innocent person to get stuck."

He sat down again. His voice was gentle. "Before I came here a long time ago, Andy, before I came down and passed the Florida bar and started a practice here, I was a smart young assistant in the District Attorney's office in—well, where it happened doesn't make any difference. I got my big chance in a murder trial. The man handling it took sick. I took over in mid-trial. I got the jury just where I wanted them, and I got the verdict I wanted, the verdict the whole office wanted because it was cruel, vindictive, premeditated murder, as callous as anything you ever expect to see. They electrocuted the guy. A real unwholesome-type guy. He yelped about innocence right up until they put the hood on him. I was so young I even wanted to see it. I was so young I was proud of myself. Eight months afterward, in connection with another case, we received a confession in such detail, containing things that hadn't even come out in the trial, that we knew we'd made a little slip. We'd sort of accidentally electrocuted the wrong fella. My friends slapped me on the back and told me it was tough luck, could have happened to anyone. I kept seeing the way my pigeon had stiffened when the current hit him. I saw that picture a lot of times, and through the bottoms of a lot of glasses. And finally I knew I'd have to do my straightening out some other place, so I came down here. And so I know it is childish and stupid to keep thinking that innocence will out. It will, usually. But any man can be an exception."

I waited in the long hot silence, and then I said, "O.K., Steve. I'll take this seriously."

"You better."

The jailer fumbled with the door, and Wargler came in. Steve said, "Bob, I thought you told me I could have all the time I wanted."

Wargler didn't even seem to hear him. He looked dumb and numbed and baffled and faintly sick. He said, "Son, shove over. I got to sit down a minute."

He sat down and we stared at him. He cracked his big knuckles. "What's wrong?" Steve demanded.

Wargler stirred and looked at him. "I guess maybe we'll let this boy go, come to think of it."

"How come?" I asked, wondering why the skin on the back of my neck had started to crawl.

"Well, dead low tide come about quarter to ten this morning. It's a slow tide right now, and those Hoover brothers, they like to net in the pass right on the tide change. They got to move fast and catch it just right, because if the tide starts to come in on 'em, they can lose a lot of net. They made the swing and they start drawing the circle tight against the Horseshoe Key side of the pass and they come up with a body. They rush it right in and get hold of me, and to hell with the fish. Strangled. I can tell that right off. Strangled and tossed in the channel in the bay someplace, and tossed in, I guess, five minutes earlier and it would have gone right through the pass and out into the Gulf."

He turned to me and he laid his hand on my knee with a surprising gentleness. "It was that big girl, son. That Hallowell girl. That big blonde works over to Wilburt's."

I guess I stood up. Anyway, I got over to the window somehow, and I was looking down through the diamond pattern at the main drag, at the sun winking on the parked cars. Monday morning and the town had a more purposeful look than yesterday, yet there was still a look of marking time about it. The sticky summer, the lack of tourists. Two little girls, too young for school, were walking hand in hand down the sidewalk, lapping delicately with their tongues at tall pink ice-cream cones.

There was a picture of Christy, gold-molten in the sun, on that afternoon of love and laughter. Afternoon of the shared cigarette. And Christy, sitting on my kitchen table, brown knees greased with Ray-pell. Christy's lips and her tears, and that thin, shy, metallic voice coming over Wargler's machine.

When we'd had the glooms, we'd helped each other. She liked gin, and fine piano, and lots of sun.

I'd walked her right into it. I'd walked her throat into whatever had closed around it. Big, casual, vibrant, unself-conscious body, drifting down the channel, bumping along the bottom in the tide current, turning with hair afloat in the current, startling the little fishes into quick darts of silver.

I put my fists on the high sill of the window and ground my eyes down against my fists until the world was full of flashing greens and purples. But I couldn't rub her out of my eyes or out of my heart. It was a hell of a time to find out that I had loved her.

Finally I became aware of a hand on my shoulder. I turned and it seemed to take long seconds to recognize Steve.

He said, "I told Bob some of the other stuff, and he says it's O.K. to leave. Want to get out of here?"

"O.K. to leave?"

"Yes. Come on."

Seemingly without transition, I was standing in the Chief's office, threading my belt through the loops. I sat down and worked the laces into my shoes. I think Steve walked with me for a while as I headed for my car. I think he was trying to tell me something or ask me something. I don't know what it was. Then he was gone and I sat in the car wondering why it wouldn't start. I looked in through the big plate-glass window. The office was empty. I found my keys finally and put the ignition key in the switch. I didn't want to go look at her. I didn't know where she was. I didn't want to find out where she was. I didn't want to see, on her face, that look of remote dignity and humility I had seen on John

Long's face. Christy was gone and there was no purpose in looking at what was left. The strong golden body was empty of her now. That body had given her pain and given her pleasure. I had seen her going down a corridor, with a strong swing of round brown legs and a swirl of skirt, and the look of her blonde hair against the green blouse and her quick parting look as she reached the end of the corridor.

I got the stubborn car started and drove back through the noon sunshine to my place, not looking at where Christy had lived as I went by. I parked and went through to the bedroom, stripped off the clothes, which had a jail smell on them, and lay across my bed.

No smart chatter, Andy boy? No winsome remarks? No banter at all? Come on. Make with the gay philosophies, the witty sayings, I thought.

It had been under my nose and I hadn't known it. Under my nose, and I had never realized I was that unknown guy walking around shot with luck.

So I cried. Shut my teeth on my wrist and cried. Like for candy they took away. Like for no more Saturdays. Like for bright life going like a train into a gray tunnel. It pulled all my nerve ends out through my skin and left me for dead. I slept then.

Something goes wrong and usually you sleep and wake up and at first you are aware that the world is not right, and you try to think what, and it all comes breaking over you like a wave. But it wasn't like that this time. I had gone to sleep with the clean knowledge of loss. It was with me while I slept. And I woke up instantly aware of the precise extent of my loss.

When I woke up it was three-thirty and Jack Ryer was standing by my bed, hands on his hips, cigarette in the corner of his mouth. I moved my legs over and he sat down on the corner of the foot of the bed, eyes steady.

"How are you making it?"

"Not good."

"You don't look good. I wouldn't want to run into those eyes in a dim alley."

"Does it show that much?"

"Enough so I'm telling you to watch it. Let Wargler operate. He has his dull moments. At times he's a little childish. But he eventually gets where he's going. Right now he wants to know where she was tossed in. Time of death was between midnight and two this morning. Slow tides, and he's been working it out and figuring, and he is pretty sure she could have been dumped in the creek right here at about twelve-thirty and ended up in the pass right at dead low tide. He knows the area and the waters better than you or I will ever know them. I came out with him. He and George are questioning everybody who lives at this layout, one at a time. When you feel like it, he wants you over there."

"Where is he?"

"At Christy's place."

"He can come here if he wants me."

"You're a big boy now, Andy. You can go over there."

"Why are you riding me? Is this the time and place for that kind of thing?" I was aware, again, of the coldness of his eyes above the rather unexpectedly sweet smile.

"When you feel like it, the Chief said." He got up,

squashed out his butt in the glass ashtray on the windowsill, and walked out. I heard the screen door bang behind him. It was an empty sound in the house.

After a while I got up and showered and put on fresh clothes, and dumped the jail-worn stuff in the laundry hamper. I was going to see Mary Eleanor. I was going to see Joy Kenney. But first the Chief was going to see me.

I didn't let my mind run ahead of me and imagine what it would be like to be in her place. I just took it a step at a time. Ardy Fowler sat on her steps. His hands, coiled and knotted from fifty years of hammer and saw and chisel and plane, rested on his blue-jeaned knees. And tears, which he was perhaps unaware of, ran out of the clear blue carpenter eyes.

He looked up at me, and said sternly, "Goddamn it, Andy. Oh, damn it all."

"I know."

He was quite fierce. "But you don't know! You don't know anything. I got old bones and tired old muscles. I get myself into bed, and God, it feels good. Got tired of waiting for her to come back and tell me how you were. Wanted to find out if I could come see you. It got late. I went to bed, but I wasn't asleep. Then I heard the bus on the way out from town, heard the air brakes hissing on it, and heard it start up again. I stuck my head around the window frame and I looked out, and she came walking down the road in the moonlight, walking slow like she was thinking. I wanted to know how you were doing in that jail. I sat right up there in bed and I was tired. A bed feels so damn good to an old man. So I lay back down and think morning time is good enough, and nobody can do anything this time of night. All I had to do was go talk to her. And the animal that got her would have run."

"Take it easy, Ardy. He would have just waited until you came back to bed."

"Maybe not. Maybe it wouldn't have been that way. Maybe that animal would have gone and found himself some other girl, somebody I—I don't know. That George fella told me about it. They were thinking there was a connection. You know, with that John Long murder. But the doc says she was attacked, too, and when that animal found out he killed her, he just dumped her in the creek, so there isn't any connection, maybe. Just something got her—something that shouldn't be running around loose."

He sat looking hopelessly toward the creek, and I went on into the familiar room. Elly, looking ten years older, got up and edged by me and left, not looking at me.

Wargler had set up the card table. Christy and I had played gin on that table all day long one Sunday in August, when the rain sounded as if it had finally decided to wash away all the land, and all the works of man. There was a lingering fragrance of her in the room, Effluvium of girl, spiced faintly with Ray-pell. Like every healthy, well-adjusted young animal, she had been clean as new dimes. Scrub and soak and scrub some more. And it made me think of that time during our brief affair, that laughing time we had taken showers together, and got into crazy awkwardnesses, and laughed at the absurdities, and ignored the hard roar of the water against us, her blonde hair pasted flat to her head, and I thought of what a damn fool I had been to think because we could laugh at our own love play that therefore it wasn't love; that love had to be something solemn, moody—a sweet dying torture.

I ached to have her back. For five seconds. Alive for just five seconds so I could tell her what I had learned about myself on this day. And for just long enough so I could ask her if she had known, all along.

Wargler said, "I got a different slant on this here thing, McClintock. I don't figure this is tied up with John."

And I knew that was exactly what I wanted him to think. I wanted him snuffing along another trail.

"So do I report back to the cell?"

"By God, if Steve and Jack hadn't give me proof that little Long woman lied flat out to me, you'd be right back there now. I want you where I can grab you any time I put my mind to it, hear?"

"O.K."

"And you better not go wandering around where anybody can get you cornered too easy. Lot of people in this town that liked John want to string you up by the thumbs and slip the hide off you, real gentle. Don't give 'em any chances at you."

"What are you doing about finding Christy's killer?"

"Son, I know my work. Sex crimes have an MO, same as other kinds. There's central files we can use. Now just stay to hell out of my way, but not too far away."

It suited me perfectly. It was dandy. It was candy and cream. But I had to look dull and disinterested, even though little wires were jerking at all my muscles.

I got into my car and drove away from there. I needed gas. I stopped at a gas station, and while the tank was being filled up I used the phone to call Mary Eleanor. The maid said in a hushed voice that she was in, but she'd taken medicine and she was sleeping and she left orders not to wake her up for anything.

That could wait a bit. That could wait and I could antici-pate it. The gas station man gave me my change and did a double take as he looked at me. As I drove out, he was hustling toward the phone. Big deal—escaped murderer.

I had a vague idea where Taylor Street was. I was right about the general area, but about three streets off. Eighty-nine was a frame house that looked as if it had been picked up bodily out of some small Indiana town in 1914 and moved to Florida. Two stories and two stunted gables, and a deep front porch with rocking chairs, and brick front steps. That happens sometimes. People retire, and distrust the unfamiliar. So they come down here and duplicate the awkward living they have endured during all the years of working and saving. Tired boxlike rooms and overstuffed furniture with crocheted dinguses on the backs and arms of the chairs. Ferns in pots, and two floors and an attic. There is a way to live in Florida—a way of turning a house inside out, so there is no real transition between outdoors and indoors. Glass and vistas and the good breeze coming through. Tile and glass and plastic, so there is nothing to absorb the dampness and sit and stink in dampness.

But they come down and build their high-shouldered houses with the tiny windows, and thus what should be a good life turns into one long almost unbearable summer in Indiana.

I parked and went up and pushed the bell and looked through the screen into a dark hallway. All the shades were down, of course. Summer in Indiana. All that was missing was the lemonade. A small sagging woman came out of one of the rooms, trotting like a weary little horse.

"Yes, yes?"

"Is Miss Kenney in, please?"

Prim lips tightened. "There's been so much coming and

going, I wouldn't know, young man. I've given up trying to keep track. You can go on up if you want to and find out. Those stairs are too much for me in this kind of weather. I suppose you've been here before, young man."

"No, I haven't."

"Go right up the stairs and go back to the end of the hall toward the bathroom, and it's the door on the left, the last door before you get to the bathroom. And please be quiet. Mr. Grimsbach works nights this week."

She gave me another look of sharp, birdlike disapproval, and trotted back to her dim warm-damp cave, no doubt to fan herself and rock and think of Indiana.

The stairs were carpeted and they creaked. I went up and walked down the carpeted hall, which also creaked. The bathroom was done in pink and blue. The lid of the john seat was down, and it was covered with some kind of knitted thing like a tea cozy, which matched the oval rug on the linoleum floor.

Her door was closed. I knocked and waited. There was no answer. I called her name softly. No answer. Mr. Grimsbach worked nights. And he snored days. I could hear him, somewhere close at hand. I turned the knob and pushed the door open.

It was done in Grand Rapids colonial maple, with a high bed, a rag rug, a big-chested bureau, a single window, a straight chair, a rocker with needlepoint. It was extremely neat and hotter than homemade sin.

Joy Kenney sat on the straight chair. She sat looking at the wall beyond the bed. She wore brief gray corduroy shorts, a white terry-cloth halter. Her feet were bare. She sat with her knees close together, her hands resting in her lap. I shut the door and spoke to her. She did not move or turn. I could see the slow lift and fall of her breathing. The room was so hot that her body was shiny with sweat and her hair was damp at the temples. I went over and shook her gently by the shoulder. She did not respond. I looked into her eyes. The pupils were tiny, expressionless.

Eleven

I SAT ON THE BED where I was within her line of vision, but she still seemed to be looking beyond me. I spoke her name a half-dozen times. It made me think of the game we used to play when we were kids. Any move or twitch or word or giggle and you lost. You had to be just like a statue. She was playing it well—too damn well. I wondered if she were drugged. It didn't seem very likely, the erect way she was sitting. An alarm clock made a busy ticking in the room. A distant car horn blasted. Grimsbach snored. And she looked through me.

I stood in front of her and slapped her across the cheek, harder than I had meant to. Her eyes seemed to narrow slightly. The blow had turned her head a bit, so that now she looked more toward the foot of the bed. She did not turn her head back to its original position. Something was nibbling at the back of my mind, an old, old memory. Suddenly it came back. A little blondie at Syracuse. The other girls in the house where she lived said she'd been acting odd and thoughtful and secretive for weeks. So all at once she moved the rest of the way out of life—moved off into some dark place of negation. And I heard at the infirmary that the doctor who examined her picked up her arm and held it high over her head. When he released it, it remained there in position until he pulled it down again. Life had become, somehow, unbearable for her, so the mind had decided to get the hell out. Catatonic dementia praecox.

I slapped her again and again. My fingers left livid marks on her cheeks. It sickened me. I had to have some way to shock her out of it, some way to bring her back to the world. I wondered if I could shock her into self-awareness through modesty, through shame. I pulled the terry-cloth halter down from her breasts, so that it was around her diaphragm, below her breasts. There was no reaction. None at all. In a way it was more sickening than the act of slapping her. I pulled the halter up awkwardly. This was something for a doctor. It occurred to me that I might be making it worse, that through my actions I might be pushing her farther and farther back into that world where she had retreated from reality.

There were two suitcases in the closet. I went through those carefully and through each drawer in the bureau.

I found the envelope Mary Eleanor had described. I found it almost by accident. It was under the paper lining in the bottom of the bottom drawer, and when I was replacing her clothing in the drawer my fingers brushed against the irregularity. In my haste to see what was in the envelope, I left the drawer open, left her clothing spilled on the floor beside the drawer. I took the envelope over to the bed. It was the kind with string wound around and around a little fiber button.

I had seen pictures like those before. A friend of mine brought some home from Japan. But the prints hadn't been very clear. He was quite delighted with them—and I thought at the time that it was a case of arrested development. I guess when I was a high-school sophomore such pictures might have given me delightful shivers and lurid dreams. But at man's estate you outgrow your pleasure in vicarious sex, even the crazed and twisted and grotesque varieties exemplified in the fourteen glossy black-and-white eight-by-ten prints I laid out on the bed.

There can be beauty in the coupling of man and woman, but only in the hearts and souls of the participants. It is not, one can readily understand, a spectator sport. We are the hairless beasts, and in our spermatic strainings there is, from a spectator standpoint, only that sort of curious interest felt by men with big bellies and tiny minds—the men who attend smokers and compensate thus for their own nocturnal inadequacies.

In nine of the fourteen prints, Mary Eleanor's face was clear and unmistakable. The camera had been directly above the well-illuminated arena. In those nine her expression was uniformly that of savage and blinded intentness, of spasmed need. In the other five she was less recognizable. The male was a well-constructed animal. And it was clear that his forte was inventiveness rather than tenderness.

I could guess at his expression. It would be one of remoteness and mild contempt. But I could only guess. In every picture a scissored slash came in from the margin at a place where it would not hurt the action, and cut his head out, so that there was a hole in every picture but one. In that one, his head had been out of range.

They were sick scenes, like the imaginings that sometimes float up out of the stagnant pools in the dark valleys of your mind. They were that ultimate evil which denies and almost refutes the existence of the human soul. They bore that same relation to love that heroin bears to red wine.

I gathered them together and slipped them back into the brown envelope. I was very willing at that moment to resign from the human race. I looked at the still face of Joy Kenney. I left the envelope on the bed and searched again. There seemed to be nothing personal in the room. No letters, no papers, none of the little bits and scraps of life that we seem to collect.

I knew that I would send someone to look after her. I went to the door and looked back at her. It seemed callous to leave her sitting there, even though I doubted whether she was aware of anything around her. I went back and picked her up and put her on the bed. She lay for a moment, and then made the first independent action. She was on her side. She pulled her knees up high, and put her chin down, and brought her doubled fists up close under her chin. I recognized the position then. It is the position of the foetus in the dark warm womb. It is the final negation of life. It is the retreat which seems one step farther away than death, because there is, in it, the implication that life had never existed.

I took the envelope and went out into the hall and closed the door after me. After her room, the hallway seemed cool. The sweat on my body was cool. The backs of my hands prickled. I tiptoed past the gargling rhythms of Mr Grimsbach, and down the creaking Indiana stairs and across the lemonade porch and back into Florida, out of the world of knitted things, and out of that sense of sweet warm horror that Bradbury seems to know so well.

The envelope lay on the car seat beside me. I wanted to know more about the pictures. I wondered if John Long had found them and taken them, and if they had, for a time, been locked in his office desk. I wondered what it would do to that man to look at such pictures. What would it do to his soul, and his dreams and his appraisal of his marriage?

I thought of Homer Prosser. His dark narrow shop would still be open. Homer has very little interest in human beings. He is concerned only with how best to capture, in a studio print, the look of sea-grape shadows on white sand, or the look of the water in a tide pool. His eyes are lenses, his fingers are acid stained—developing fluid flows in his veins.

I was able to park right in front of his camera shop. Two women were buying film. Prosser's anemic daughter was waiting on them. She recognized me and for a moment her eyes almost came alive. When I asked for Homer she said he was in the back.

I went back and knocked.

"Who is it?" he asked in his thin voice.

"McClintock, Homer. Busy?"

He opened the door and looked vaguely at me. "Fixing something. What do you want?"

He backed away as I came in. I pulled the door shut. "Homer, I want you to look at some pictures and tell me everything you can about how they were made, and I want you to forget you ever saw them."

His eyes slid to the envelope. "Prints? It's hard to tell much from prints. A little. Not much."

"And forget you saw them?"

"If you say so."

The thought of a technical problem brought him alive. He took the envelope and went over to a long table and switched on a bright light and took the prints out of the envelope. He looked at them, one by one, as calmly as a grocer inspecting lettuce. He picked two and put them down side by side and put the rest in the envelope.

"Competent," he said. "Professional, or very good amateur. From the definition of the shadows—here and, see, over here—I'd guess it might be infrared. Illumination would be a very pretty problem. From the shadows there was a light source over here, and one over here, probably. Camera always in the same place. Same focus, same aperture."

"Infrared?" I asked.

"Take pictures in what seems to be total darkness. Just that the wave length of the light used is out of the range of the human eye. Film can pick it up, though. Very fast film, wide aperture, relatively long exposure. Movement is a little blurred in a couple of these. Used to be pretty rare. Amateurs have been doing it in the last few years. Naturalists. So on."

"Then they wouldn't know a picture was being taken?"

"Oh, no. Look to them like a dark room. Brightly lighted, though, as far as the camera is concerned. The photography in these is better than the developing. Sort of a fast careless job there." He slid the two prints in with the others and, turning in the chair, handed me the envelope. "Sorry, that's all I can tell you."

"That's enough, Homer. What do I owe you?"

He stared uncomprehendingly at me. "I didn't do anything."

When I went back out after thanking him, a couple of the town hard boys were leaning against my car, pale-eyed, tensed up, trying to look casual as all hell. I couldn't remember their names. They had both worked on jobs of ours off and on. They fished commercial a little, went cat hunting in the sloughs in season, took illegal gators when they could find a market.

"How you doin', lady killer?" the biggest one asked.

"Suicided anybody lately?" the other one asked.

The biggest one was leaning against the car door. He had his arms crossed in such a way that his fists bulged his big brown biceps. I wanted no part of a street brawl and that was what they had in mind. I could smell it.

"You boys want something?" I asked mildly.

"We want to know how come they let you out?"

"Yeah, you must have given old Wargler a lot of your smart talk. Old John Long was a right good friend of mine. And we don't go for people playing around with other people's women. Somebody ought to take a fish knife and fix you up so you stay out of trouble."

You work in the town and so you are a part of the community, and then all of a sudden you're just as much a stranger as when you first arrived, indistinguishable from any tourist.

"What you got there?" the big one asked, looking at the envelope. "Pardon from the governor? Let me see that."

He held his hand out. I said, "No. You can't see what I've got here, boys. It's private business."

The smaller one moved out a bit, casually, moving slowly, with the very obvious intention of coming around behind me. I moved back onto the sidewalk to keep them both in front of me. It had helped them to have something specific they wanted. It was better and easier than just the vague idea of embarrassing me, of needling me and hoping something would start up. I couldn't see any U.S. Cavalry riding down the street with bugles and pennons. And either one of them could break my head.

I said adios to pride and male vanity. I spun around and ran like a rabbit. I ran better than a rabbit. I didn't waste any time bounding. I received a lot of startled looks, but I ran right on down to Saddler's Drugs and through the door and to the phones.

I remembered then what I had neglected to do, and the first person I called was Dr. Graman. His nurse got him on the line and when I recognized his precise, slightly girlish voice, I told him about Joy Kenney and gave him her address.

"Did you say McClintock?" he asked.

"Yes, I did." From the booth I could look out the front door and see my two friends standing on the corner.

"I don't understand your relationship to this girl."

"We employed her last week. I went to see why she wasn't working and found her like I told you I found her. If you don't want to touch it, who should I call?"

"Could she have had some—great emotional shock?"

"I haven't the faintest idea."

"Ah—you are—at liberty?"

"Released from jail? Yes."

"Do you want to be advised about Miss Kenney? Where can I reach you?"

"I'll get in touch with you. If she's bad off, where will you take her?"

"To the hospital right here, temporarily. There are a few

limited facilities. Do you know how to get in touch with her relatives?"

"No. From what she said there's just one brother. And I don't know where he might be."

"I'll go over right away, then."

I hung up. It was nearly five-thirty. I wondered about calling for police protection. It seemed like yelling for Mamma. But my rough friends were still out there. As I glanced toward the door I saw Steve Marinak come striding in and stop at the cashier's counter for cigarettes. He had changed shirts during the day, changed to a green and yellow and white checked job. The girl gave him his change just as I came up to him.

"Hey, Andy," he said, his red face sober and concerned.

"Come here a minute." I led him away from people over toward the magazine rack. "Those two characters out there—see them?—are waiting around to bust me on the nose. Any suggestions?"

"You aren't popular enough to be roaming around town, Andy."

"That isn't the immediate problem. Those guys are."

"Come on. I know 'em."

I followed him out. He marched up to them. "Something on your mind, boys?"

"I guess you don't care who you're seen with, hey, Steve?" the big one said.

"Boys, you better simmer down. If you got to take a punch at Andy, go ahead. I'll watch. Then when you've had your fun, I'll fix it so you lose that boat of yours, Joe. And we'll take that lot you own at Crescent Acres, Harry. First you stand still for a criminal charge of assault and battery, and then we clip you with a civil suit. If it's worth that to you, go right ahead."

They sneered. They called a few names. They swaggered off, but the tails were definitely tucked between the legs. It pleased me. Not the way I would care to win all personal combat, but a very pleasant way to do it at the moment.

Steve tore open one of the fresh packs he had bought and offered me a cigarette. As I lighted his and mine, he said, "Why don't you go back to your place and sit tight?"

"I might do that," I said.

"It might save you some fuss. You're lucky to be out. Wargler has this—Christy thing pegged as having no relationship to the other."

"What do you think?"

He looked uneasy. "Well, you told me you sent her out to look into that—broken desk thing, and check with the Kenney girl. I'm not sure. Maybe it could be either way."

"Wargler's probably right," I said.

"Maybe." He looked at me and looked away. There was a little awkwardness between us.

"Did you tell him everything I told you, Steve?"

"No. You're a client." He glanced down and seemed to notice the envelope for the first time. His eyes narrowed as he glanced up into my face. "Is that the thing Mary Eleanor lost?"

"It might be."

"What did I tell you about keeping nothing from me?"

"You told me to tell you everything, Steve."

"Is that the envelope?"

"I'll let you know."

"Who took it? The Kenney girl?"

"I couldn't say, Steve."

"Goddamn it, Andy! What are you trying to pull?"

"I'll let you know."

"I can drop the case right here and now. I don't have to take a case where the client holds out on me."

"That's right, you can drop out right now."

"Don't you care?"

"To tell the truth, I don't care a hell of a lot. I haven't cared since Wargler came into the cell this morning."

"It won't do you any good to be a damn fool. What's in the envelope?"

"I'll see you around, Steve."

He bit his lip and stared across the street for a time. Then he said, "O.K. Try it this way, then. How about a trade?"

"A trade?"

"What I know against what's in the envelope."

"Do you know anything special, Steve?"

"I know something that doesn't fit into the picture. At least I can't make it fit. In fact, it doesn't make a hell of a lot of sense to me."

"Then why should it interest me?"

"Because maybe it throws a little more light on that conversation you had Thursday morning with John."

"Suppose you tell me, Steve, and then if it is as important as what I've got right here, you can have a look."

We had been walking slowly up the street and we came to my car. The car was now in shadow, so we sat in it.

"That isn't such a hot deal," he said. "You can listen and then not show me."

"It's the only deal I'll make."

He sighed. "You're hard to get along with. O.K., here it is.

Another lawyer in town has been a little upset ever since John was killed. This afternoon he came over and told me what was on his mind. Seems that John came to see him late last Thursday afternoon and asked for some information, with the agreement in advance that the lawyer would ask no question in return. The lawyer agreed. John asked some pointed questions: What's the local deal on the unwritten law? What has happened in the past? Suppose the husband kills just the man involved? What usually happens when he kills them both? And so on. My lawyer friend said that if John were asking those questions because he had the intent to kill, then he was pretty calm about it. Like somebody who had thought it over a long time, made a tentative decision, and was just checking the legal aspects before going ahead with it. You see where that leaves me, Andy. It doesn't help your case a damn bit. If the prosecution can convince a jury you were fadiddling with Mary Eleanor, then it can be made to look as though you had to knock John off before he could jump first."

"But we can show she spread it around thoroughly."

"That's tougher than you think. A man will half promise, but when it comes to actually swearing it in court, he'll back out. I've seen it happen."

I tapped the edge of the envelope against the steering wheel. This was the place where I had to make a decision. I didn't want to get Steve so involved in it he'd get in my way. And yet I was afraid that if I didn't show him what I had, he'd get in my way in his efforts to find out. Maybe it would be better to give him something to think about.

I tossed the envelope into his lap. I didn't look at him. I heard the sound as he pulled the photographs out.

"Lord Almighty!" he said in a hushed voice.

I turned and watched him as he went through the batch. They really stunned him. He put them back in the envelope and his mouth had a twist of disgust. "My God, seeing and believing are two different things, aren't they? My God, do you think John got hold of these?"

"I don't know. From what you told me, it looks that way."

"You are completely and finally off the hook. That guy is definitely not you. My God, they'd clear the court if these had to be introduced as evidence. But with these in our pocket, they'll never try you. They wouldn't dare. My God, can you imagine being *married* to that! I'd rather live in a septic tank. And imagine her posing for them! What the hell kind of a woman is that?"

"I don't think she did. I asked Homer. He thinks they were taken with infrared lights. She'd think it was dark."

"That would make it a blackmail pitch, Andy. Who cut the heads out, I wonder?"

"Maybe the photographer. Maybe it's a double play. Maybe there's another set with her head cut out. I don't know."

"I'm keeping these, Andy."

"No, you're not."

"We can't take the chance of you losing them, of somebody taking them away from you. They're like bonds, for God's sake."

We compromised. He took seven and I took seven. He promised to go right back to his office and stow his seven in the office safe. I got the envelope along with my seven. Then I drove him to his office. He scuttled up the stairs with the photographs hugged against his shirt.

I drove on slowly. Mary Eleanor had the key to all of it. Right in her depraved little head. It wasn't going to stay there, of that I was certain. It was going to come out, and she was going to release all the keys willingly or unwillingly and the choice would be hers as to how she did it.

There is a certain set of social and environmental rules about using violence on a woman. It is not done, old boy, I told myself.

But the pictures had released me from that. I could no longer think of her as a woman. The word implies a member of the human race. Mary Eleanor had forfeited membership. She hadn't kept up her dues. Her name had been posted on the bulletin board, and they had ousted her from the club, and she wasn't entitled to sign checks any longer. And thus she no longer had the immunity of a club member. If a dog locks its teeth on your ankle, you are privileged to kick it loose from its skull.

Mary Eleanor had, somehow, set the whole thing moving. Like pushing over the first one of a row of blocks. And the last block had fallen on my Christy. Mary Eleanor and I were going to have a chat—a heart to heart. A viewing of the real art photos. A real letting down of hair.

Twelve

THE SHADOWS WERE LONG and blue and the sun was gone when I drove into Mary Eleanor's driveway. The black MG was there, looking sedate with its top up. When I turned off the motor I could hear the slow, thick sighing of the Gulf. My footsteps crackled on the shell drive. As I pressed the bell a mosquito whined by my ear and I blew smoke toward him.

The door was open. Nobody answered. I waited and then tried the latch on the screen. It was fastened. I rattled the door hard and waited. I could look through into the long low living room, out through the window wall at the slant of beach beyond the terrace.

In sudden exasperation I put my knee against the door frame, took the screen latch in both hands, and yanked hard. There was a brittle breaking sound and the screen came open and a bit of metal tinkled on the cement. I stepped into the house and let the screen close slowly behind me. I slapped the envelope of pictures against my leg.

I went through and into her bedroom. She lay facedown in a flimsy robe, and it was folded halfway up the backs of her thighs. I stood just inside the doorway. The room was dim and bluish and quite cool. I could not see her move and I could not hear her breathe.

I took three slow steps to the side of the bed and looked down at her. At that distance I could hear the soft purring sound of her breathing. I decided to shake her awake. I reached down toward her shoulder . . .

"Hold it!"

I froze for a moment and turned slowly. The bathroom door swung the rest of the way open and the husky young cop I had first seen blocking the driveway at Key Estates came toward me, his stub-barreled revolver aimed at my belt.

"Oh, McClintock. What's on your mind?"

I got the impression that he was disappointed to see me. "I want to talk to her."

"Some other time."

"It won't take long. Give me some time with her."

"Even if I could, it wouldn't do you a damn bit of good. I never see anything like it. She's been drinking all day, ever since she come back from headquarters this morning. Damn near two full quarts of bonded bourbon. You couldn't wake her up if you set her on fire."

"What are you doing here?"

"I'm staked out here."

"Waiting for somebody in particular?"

"You better get on your horse, Mr. McClintock."

"When can I talk to her alone?"

"I couldn't say. You'll have to ask the Chief."

There wasn't anything I could do. I wasn't going to get any morsels of information out of her. I went back out to my car. I sat there with the motor running for a few minutes. Joy seemed to know John Long—he seemed to know her. She had the pictures. She had suffered an emotional shock. A lot of people had been coming and going, in and out of her room. One of them could have been the man whose head was deleted from the pictures. Or the man who had taken the pictures. Steve had talked about blackmail. John had talked to another lawyer about the unwritten law. He had spoken of killing both of them. So he knew whose head had been cut out. He knew the face. Had he cut them out himself to use in order to find the guy? Had he found him? In finding him, had he run into Joy?

A lot of threads tied a lot of things together, but I couldn't detect which threads were real, and which ones were the result of too much imagination on my part.

I drove to Taylor Street. The woman trotted into the hall again, dabbing at her lips with a napkin. "Oh, it's you, young man. You won't find her this time. They took her away." She seemed to be finding considerable satisfaction in that, and in being able to tell me that.

"I wonder if you could give me some information."

"I am eating supper, young man."

"Could I wait?"

"The other man was very rude with all his questions."

"What other man?"

"The one who was here about forty minutes ago, after they took her away in the doctor's car. He was a very ignorant-looking man, and he kept writing things down and kept licking the pencil. He was a policeman. Sergeant George something. I wouldn't be surprised at anything that girl did. She was a queer one, believe me. And what am I supposed to do with her things?"

"Maybe she'll be back."

"Not to stay in my house, she won't be back. My supper is getting cold, young man."

"Can I wait in there?"

"Yes, you can, but please don't smoke as I can't get the smell out of the drapes."

I sat and waited. I could see into the empty dining room. I could hear the thin sound of her voice in the kitchen, and the deeper rumble of a man's voice, the clink of silverware on pottery. The room had an airless musty smell. The rug had a faded pattern of dragons and roses. The shade of the single lighted lamp was pink, ornate, and covered with cellophane.

She trotted in and plumped herself on the couch and bounced a few times, and said, "I suppose you'll ask all the same questions over again. Who are you, anyway?"

It was a problem. I didn't want her to run away screaming. But I couldn't delay too long. "Andrew McClintock."

"Oh, goodness! I read and heard all about you. It was extremely stupid of them to put you in jail, Mr. McClintock. I'm a good judge of character. I can tell from the shape of your head that you could never kill anybody."

"Thank you."

"If I'd known your name, I could have saved that police person some trouble. I described you in great detail and finally he grunted and scribbled in his silly little notebook. I always say if anybody wants me to know their name, they'll tell me. Of course, I knew Miss Hallowell by sight. Why in the world Wilburt can't get some new books in that loan library I'll never know."

"When was Miss Hallowell here?"

"Understand now, Mr. McClintock, I don't keep tabs on people coming and going. She was here yesterday. Sunday, it was, and I guess she was here about four in the afternoon, or maybe later. Then she went away, and that man came and he was here longer than I care to have men here in a room with a single girl. I'm not old fashioned, but I say there's a limit, and decency is decency wherever you find it. Once I get my mind made up to ask a girl to go, I do it, and that is what I was thinking on yesterday when that man was here. He left along about dark, and Miss Hallowell was back here again but she didn't stay long, and that was very late. I'd say. I went to bed and then, about an hour later, I heard Miss Kenney go down the stairs and unlock the door and I heard a man's voice down there with her, and I guess he must have gone around the side of the house and chunked a pebble on her window or something. She came back up the stairs with him, both of them walking quiet. Right then and there I made up my mind to talk to her, and tell her to get out. I lay there so mad I couldn't get to sleep and he stayed maybe ten minutes and then went real quiet back down the stairs and let himself out. I got up and went to make sure the door was latched and it was locked like it should be. I heard her in her room, making a mewly little noise like she was crying, and any normal time I'd ask a body what the trouble is, but, as I said, I'd just about give up on that girl. I was real pleased for her when she gave up that waiting table work and got a decent job in Mr. Long's office, but I tell you, that kind of girl brings trouble wherever she works. Oh, I'm not saying she isn't nice enough to speak to. So polite and nice butter wouldn't melt. But I always say these tropics can do something to nice girls to make them forget their upbringing, and forget plain decency."

She looked at me almost triumphantly and bounced up and down a little on the couch. "Do you know who the man was? The one who was here for about ten minutes?"

"Well, I certainly *hope* it was the same one who's been coming to see her, even if he is strange acting."

"What does he look like?"

"Now, it's funny, but I never have got a real good look at him. Not to talk to. I'd say he's about as tall as you. With a soft voice. And he wears a hat, and you don't see so many young men wearing hats down here. And he has kind of—well, a kind of poor look. Run-down-at-the-heels kind of look. But I swear I never had a real good chance to stare him right in the face."

"Did he come here in a car?"

"Now, you know, that's the same thing that policeman kept asking me. I know he came in a car a couple of times, and I know that once it was a little black shiny car with a cloth top, and it looked new, but it still had a sort of old-fashioned look. You know, with those wire wheels and all. And he came in another car usually, that looked more like him."

"Like him?"

"A sort of gray dusty kind of thing, the kind of car you wouldn't look at twice. I know I didn't."

"That's all you could tell the police about him."

"That's every word of it, young man."

"Miss Kenney was trying to get another job while she was working at the restaurant?"

"Yes, but you know, that's a funny thing. That agency man, he'd keep calling her up and he'd have a job for her, but she just wasn't interested at all, until this chance to work for Mr. Long came along. Then she seemed excited and upset about getting the job. Nervous, like. I suppose she was out of practice. It gave me the shivers to see them taking her out of here. My goodness, her face was empty as a bed sheet. She'd halfway walk when they pushed on her a little. I can't help feeling sorry for the poor thing, taken sick that way, even if I was all set in my mind to ask her to look for another room. I pick up the rooms myself, and it's no pleasure to have to clean up after a body who leaves sand and sand spurs on my hooked rug, and his pants cuffs and shoes always wet like he had to wade to get here, so he dripped, and mud caking off his shoes. I swear to Betsy, that man must live in a swamp. And I must say, it surprised me to see that nice Miss Hollowell coming to see Joy Kenney. Joy!" She sniffed. "Funny idea to name a girl that." She leaned forward. "But, then again, I understand that Miss Hallowell is divorced. *She* can't be any better than she has to be either. How does she get away calling herself Miss?"

"She's dead. They took her out of the bay this morning."

She leaned back on the couch, her eyes wide. "And me, with the radio turned off all day long because it just seemed too hot to listen! Oh, the poor, poor dear! How in the world did it happen?"

I stood up. "Somebody strangled her and threw her in."

"My goodness to Betsy, it's getting terrible around here. And I've been after him and after him to fix that lock on the back door. Why, if this keeps up, a body won't be safe walking the streets!"

All of a sudden I had to get out of the hot musty room, away from her little sharp fox eyes, away from her slightly sickly innuendoes.

"Thank you for the information."

"That's perfectly all right, and if you can, young man, you find out what in the world I'm supposed to do with Miss Kenney's things. I don't want her back here. Do you think it would be all right to pack them up in her suitcases? Then I could rent the room out. It's never any trouble to rent a room when you keep a nice clean house with everything spick and span."

"You better use your own judgment on that."

Before I reached the porch steps, she closed the front door, and I heard the lock snap. I got into the car and looked at the house and saw her going from window to window, fiddling with the latches.

The local hospital is inadequate. It seems as if everybody and his brother have been moving to Florida and bringing the kids. It's getting so you have to line up for everything. Schools, roads, lunch, room to fish off a bridge. It shocks you a little when you go inland about five miles and find it looking as though Señor de Leon hadn't taken his trip yet.

I hung around the front desk after being told, in chilly fashion, that Dr. Graman was inside, and that Miss Kenney was a patient. We've made quite a deal out of sickness and death. Now they're something that comes with a rustle of starch, a quick needle in the arm, a brisk smell of disinfectant, and hushed voices. And if you discourage everybody by dying, then you get a big party, with bronze handles and organ music and lavender delivery trucks from the florists. But the hole they drop you in seems to be just as deep. And you are no more aware of the ceremony than was your re-mote ancestor—the one they had to drag farther away from the cave after a while.

Thinking of death was like drilling a raw nerve. Goodby to my girl. And I stood there with the reliable heart sucking and pumping the warm red blood, the little valves working like IBM, the temperature control system supplying just enough surface evaporation to keep the organism right to a tenth of a degree, all the glands and ducts adding their two bits to the process on automatic request. The machine was working dandy, and my girl's machine had quit. I stood there oxygenating my blood stream, rebuilding tissues, picking up images through the wet eye lenses, burning stored calories, catching sounds on the taut ear diaphragms, and my girl had gone out of business. Out of the business of living. A lot of cheap sea gulls and cut-rate pelicans and shoddy Pekinese and second-grade human beings were still warm and functioning, but my Christy was flaccid and cold and unaware. I thought there'd better be that golden street and those golden slippers. They went with the bearded God of childhood, but they better be there. There better be that sweet chariot, and a gate and a book they could look her up in and say come in. Maybe she'd sit in the anteroom, and say, "Thanks. I'm just waiting."

Graman came striding busy-like down the hall and when he saw me a look of mild distaste clouded his pretty face. "Oh, hello there."

"How is she, Doctor?"

"Completely unresponsive. I tried adrenalin. That will sometimes break the catatonic state when it is the result of emotional shock. I thought for a time it would work. She however merely spoke irrationally for a few seconds and then

150   JOHN D. MACDONALD

lapsed back. Dr. Vayse will look in later tonight. It's more in his line. I'm not even positive of diagnosis, much less prognosis, McClintock."

"What did she say when she was irrational?"

He stared at me. "Why? Nothing of importance, certainly. Something about a barn and a kitten. They often revert to childhood."

"Doctor, it might be important. Can you repeat it?"

"Really; I—"

"Please."

He sighed. "Something like this: 'You see, I knew kitty had to be in the barn. He liked it there. He always went there. That's why I looked there first, and he hadn't even covered her up. She should have been covered up. Shouldn't she have been covered up? It was just a little thing to do that.' Does that satisfy you?"

"That's all she said?"

"You'll have to forgive me, McClintock. I have other patients." He went over and moved the wooden peg beside his name to show that he wasn't in the hospital, and walked out into the night.

After a time I followed him. I was a big operator. I stood by my car wondering what to do next. I was real shrewd. Two women to talk to, and both of them had slid out of reach—one had gone down the greased skid called bourbon, and the other had fallen off some personal precipice. It brought me back to the only tangible thing I had—those pictures. I sat in the car and took the feeble flashlight from the glove compartment and studied them carefully, one by one, looking this time at the setting rather than the characters. It gave me one corner of a night stand, a bit of wall that seemed to be plaster, a small hunk of lamp shade. The man wore a wristwatch. It was quite clear in one picture. Clear enough so a jeweler could tell the make. I put them back in the envelope and sat in the dark and smoked.

Thirteen

AFTER WHAT SEEMED to be a long time, my brain began to work in a slightly more logical fashion. The pictures had been taken for a purpose. That purpose was undoubtedly profit. It would do no good to try to squeeze money out of John Long with any threat to show the pictures to the wrong people. But the complete set, or even any one of them, was a wonderful crowbar with which to extract funds from Mary Eleanor. A shrewd operator would give her one set of prints, as food for thought. Mary Eleanor had foolishly let the pictures get away from her. Keeping them was perhaps an evidence of her disease.

O.K. so far. Now then, Mary Eleanor had certainly been in no doubt as to the identity of her partner. So what would be served by the blackmailer's cutting the partner's face out of the pictures? That didn't make sense. It didn't make a bit of sense. And it didn't make any sense to think of Mary Eleanor cutting those heads out of the pictures. She wouldn't want to put them in lockets.

I began to feel a faint surge of excitement. O.K. I'm John Long. Maybe I've had a vague idea for some time that friend wife is a shade on the tramp side. She takes too many trips alone. I'm not the sort of guy who would catch on very fast, but I've begun to have my doubts. So I keep my eyes open. And I sort of poke around when I get a chance. Maybe the next time she goes away, I really give her room a good search. She had the pictures hidden well, but I found them. And I sat on the bed and I looked at my wife and I put the pictures down carefully and went in the bathroom and threw up and came back and looked at them some more. She was away, and it was a good thing because if she had been handy I would have killed her with my hands right then and there. But I am the kind of guy who goes at things doggedly and thoroughly. It took me a lot of years to get around to doing Key Estates, and I made myself wait until I could do it well. I sat and looked at the pictures of the thing I had called wife. And I looked at the man. I had never seen him before. That bothered me. And it meant he was probably from out of town. I wondered whether to put the pictures back where I had found them, and wait. But that meant I might never get my hands on him. So I went over to the bureau and took her scissors and cut the heads out of the pictures. His head. I've got too much pride to show the whole picture around. These were mailed from Miami. I can take these crudely cut out heads and I can send them to a firm of private investigators in Miami and I can ask them to find out who the man is—and where he is. But that means I can't leave the mutilated pictures here. So I'll take them and lock them in my desk at the office. Let her look for them and sweat. I'm over my first anger and outrage now, and I can wait, and in my own good time I'll kill them both quite dead because of what looking at these pictures has just done to me.

It made very good sense to me, as I sat there in the car. Take it another step. John Long *had* found out who the man was, and where he was. And, having found him, and having quietly investigated his own legal status, he found himself caught right in the middle. If he went ahead, he would be put out of circulation and Key Estates would come to a standstill. And Key Estates had been his baby. Yet, it would take a long time to finish it off, and during that time he had to live with the diseased soul-sick wife-thing. Then up steps that young McClintock, and John Long cussed himself for not having seen earlier how it could be handled so that both the things he had to do were accomplished. First I had thought he was sick and going to die. Next I had thought somebody was going to kill him and he knew it. The third and inevitable answer was that he was going to kill somebody else—and that act would take him out of circulation just as certainly as his own death.

The device of trying to put myself inside his mind had worked so well that I decided to try Mary Eleanor's.

O.K. I am an insatiable tramp. I don't care what I do or with whom. I was having a fine and dandy time, and then— Joe trapped me. I don't know how the damn pictures were taken, but they were taken and there's no mistake about that. It is certainly hideous to see yourself like I am in those pictures. I thought he was kidding, and I laughed at him when he said he had pictures. Then he sent me a set, right through the mail. First I wanted to kill myself, and then I wanted to kill him, and then I knew that he'd grabbed me and I couldn't get out of it and I had to do just what he told me to do, or, like he said, my dull husband would get a complete set in the mail. And that would be a death sentence. John is slow and stolid, but he has so much pride he would have to kill me to get himself halfway clean again if he ever saw those pictures.

I should have thrown them away, burned them. I know that now. God knows why I kept them around. They were safe, I thought. I guess I liked the danger of having them around. And every few weeks, I'd take them out and look at them again. Once I got over the first nasty impression, I found that it could get me sort of excited, looking at them, so I kept them around.

And then I came home and found they were gone. I was frantic. I wanted to pack up and run. Then I thought maybe the maid had found them. It was a slim chance. But John acted queer—damn queer. He wouldn't talk to me. He wouldn't touch me. So I knew he had them. I knew he had looked at them and I could almost guess what it had done to him. I was horribly frightened of what he would do, and the weeks went by and he didn't do anything, and I began to get my courage back, thinking that maybe he would never do anything. Then I guessed that he must be trying to find out who Joe is. And the envelope being mailed from Miami and all.

I told Joe about it, and he was angry. He said I should have burned them. John acted so strange. I talked McClintock into finding out what John was thinking. I thought John might give him a hint. I couldn't understand his doing nothing. And then Andy McClintock told me what John had said. He didn't know what it meant. I did. It meant he knew who

Joe was, meant that he had made up that slow ponderous mind of his, meant that now he was ready, or would soon be ready, to kill us. As soon as McClintock was trained. There was no one to turn to. No one but Joe. I told him right away. He questioned me. He asked me about McClintock. I didn't know what he was planning. He took that spear thing from McClintock's house. I don't know how he got John to meet him out there at Key Estates, or how he managed to surprise him. It was all like a game, somehow. And it didn't hit me until I heard the words, until I heard Andy say John was dead. He came to me, Joe did, after Andy was arrested. He told me that I had to lie, that I had to protect myself, because I was involved too. And I asked Andy to get the pictures. Where are the pictures? Who has them? Who has looked at them and found out what I am? I can't help it. I never could help it. But who knows? I wish John were alive. I want him back, now. There is nothing left to do but chase it out of my mind. With bourbon. Stop thinking and feeling and living for a while.

There were still a lot of holes, but it had form now.

I called the mystery man Joe. It made it simpler. He had gone to Taylor Street once in a car that had to be Mary Eleanor's. It had to be the same man. That made Joy Kenney an accomplice. Two harpies. They'd found a couple to feed on—the Longs. Emotional shock. She hadn't wanted him to go that far—not as far as murder. She had lucked her way into a job in John's office. Moving in close to where the money is. I understood more of her tension and her nervousness.

Joe. Man without a head. Shabby, soft-voiced, wearing a

hat. Damp pants cuffs and shoes. Sand and sand spurs. An anonymous automobile.

Why shabby? Why anonymous? Hadn't he made Mary Eleanor pay off?

And that one question gave me a place to go, and gave me something to do.

Harvey Constanto is a pallid, formless, drifting kind of man. He is the kind you put on obscure committees where the real work is done. Nobody ever slaps his shoulder, and if he hears a dirty joke, it is because he is drifting around the fringe of a group that happens to be exchanging same. His smile is uncertain, his manner half apologetic. It is inconceivable that he could have ever wooed and won his brown, loud, boisterous, flirtatious, popular wife, much less bed her down. Yet there are three handsome healthy teenage kids with Harvey's unmistakable sharp nose. It is insane to think of Harvey being aggressive, yet he started with nothing, and now owns heavy swatches of the best Gulf-front property.

When I rang their bell, Harvey came and peered at me through the screen in his lean near-sighted way, and said, "Oh, Mr. McClintock. How do you do. Won't you come in? Ah—please come in, won't you?"

"Thanks."

"Ah—Marian is out and I haven't seen any of the children around, so they must be out, too. Would you—ah—care for a drink?"

"No, thanks, Mr. Constanto. This is—well, a business matter, I guess you'd call it."

"Then come right in here. This is my den."

He turned on the desk lamp. It wasn't what I would call a

den. It looked as austere as his office in the bank. He sat un-
certainly behind the desk and put his sharp elbows on the
desk.

"I suppose," he said, "it is something about John. A tragic
loss to the community, Mr. McClintock. Tragic. A very—
ah—old and beloved friend. You understand, of course, that
I'm not authorized to give you confidential information. Financial affairs. That sort of thing."

"This isn't directly about John's financial affairs, Mr. Constanto. I have reason to believe that someone has been black-
mailing Mary Eleanor. I thought you might help me confirm
that by telling me—off the record, of course—whether she
had access to any money."

"Couldn't you ask her?"

"People being blackmailed don't talk too readily."

"How does it become your business?"

"You can't live in this town without knowing that I was
jailed, released, and I'm still under suspicion. I think the
blackmail ties in with the murder. And I'm interested in
clearing myself."

"Why not go to the police and let them investigate?"

"And find out why and how Mary Eleanor was being
blackmailed and make it public? Get it in the papers and over
the radio, maybe?"

"I—ah—see. A certain moral responsibility."

He then looked me directly in the eyes. I knew at once that
it had never happened to me before, and I guessed also that
he seldom looked anybody directly in the eye. His eyes were
a singularly pale clear cold blue, and they were as merciless as
bookkeeping machinery, or a tax table. He looked away

quickly, but once you had looked into those eyes you understood a lot of things. How the brown wife was won. Why
the kids were exceptionally well behaved. How, precisely, he
had come up from nothing. You saw how much there was
behind that vagueness, how much ambition and arrogance
and cold willfulness.

He made a tent of his fingers. "You—ah—understand
that if I had known her reason, I would never have assisted
her."

"Of course."

"Her security, naturally was her stock in John Long, Contractors, Incorporated. Not listed, of course. Not readily
marketable. She was evasive as to why she needed the money.
She led me to assume that it was for a purchase of land. Speculative, of course. To be a surprise to her husband. Something like that. She wished to use her holdings as collateral
for a bank loan. However, I explained to her that it could not
be kept a secret from her husband in that case, as he was a
director of the bank, and all loans of the size of what she had
in mind have to be taken up at the meetings. If John did not
happen to attend that one, he would certainly hear about it.
That upset her. Then I—ah—suggested, purely as a favor, of
course, an alternate suggestion."

"What was that?"

"I agreed to loan her the money she required, and accept a
temporary assignment of the stock holdings as collateral for
a personal loan, which no one had to know about, of course.
It was—ah—handled in that manner. It took me several days
to raise what she required in cash. Thirty thousand. A month
later she required another ten. I managed that for her. About

a month ago she wanted ten more. I told her I had gone as far as I cared to go on that amount of collateral. She was more than a bit—unpleasant about it."

"If she was paying off someone, she couldn't hope to repay the loan, then."

"I don't see how she could. I imagine it was a case of either letting me become the owner of the holding, or else informing John. Of course now she'll have no trouble. After taxes there'll be a decent estate. In fact a—ah—small group of which I am one plan to make a firm offer for John's controlling interest in the firm. That Key Estates project looks healthy—quite healthy. John planned well. A pity he couldn't live to see it completed."

"Mr. Constanto, I would think that if you were such a good friend of John's, you'd have told him about his wife wanting all that money in cash."

The blue eyes swung on their turrets and aimed at me and for a moment I thought he was going to fire when ready, but he turned, instead, to vagueness, to his apologetic manner. He said, "Ah, in retrospect, yes. We're always—wise, after the fact, aren't we?"

You couldn't pin him down any further, any more than you can drive nails with a wet dishrag. It was obvious that he'd been delighted to buy for forty thousand a thirty per cent interest in a healthy firm that stood to net a very chubby figure from Key Estates. He was an admired and respected local citizen, and yet he gave me the same feeling you get when you run your face through a cobweb.

"I appreciate your telling me this, Mr. Constanto."

"Once you stated your interest, I felt it was my moral obligation to inform you, Mr. McClintock. I hope it will—assist you in your difficulties."

He walked me gravely and politely to the door. He said, "Perhaps it would be wise for me to give the police the same information, Mr. McClintock. I should not like to be accused of withholding information that might be of interest to them. Yet, by the same token, I do not wish to cause Mrs. Long any—any difficulty."

"Why don't you wait a day or so?"

"If you—ah—recommend it, I shall."

When I drove away I saw him, tall, stooped, framed in the doorway. He would fix your drink, carry your bundles, call you a cab, cash your check, buy your lunch. He was a very obliging kind of man. You were always seeing his name in the paper—as pall bearer.

Now Joe had another facet. Forty thousand dollars had been added.

Fourteen

IT WAS AFTER NINE, and I felt vaguely uncomfortable and couldn't decide why until I remembered that breakfast was the only meal I'd had. On impulse I drove out to the restaurant where Joy had worked.

I guess every state in the country is infected with them—greasy-spoon restaurants on the fringe of town. Red imitation leather, badly cracked, on the counter stools. Weary pie behind glass. A stink of frying grease in front, and tired garbage in back. Sway-backed, heavy-haunched waitresses with metallic hair, puffed ankles, and a perennial snarl. A decent toss of one of the water glasses would fell a steer. A jukebox and plastic booths and today's special is chicken croquettes, with fr. fr. pot. and st. beans—ninety-fi' cents. And the coffee is like rancid tar.

There were a couple of morose men, who looked like unsuccessful salesmen, sitting at the counter shoveling burned

fat into their maltreated stomachs. I sat in a booth. Their evening rush, if any, had cleared out. Three waitresses sat in a
booth. One of them got up reluctantly and slobbed over to
me and tossed a menu in front of me.

She was a slat thin blonde with improbable breasts, which
looked as real as a display soda in a drugstore window. She
had a hacksaw face and mean little eyes.

I tried to smile at her, and said, "Is Joy around?"

"Her—she quit. She's gone back into office work. She's
smart. She got off her feet. You want something?"

I found one item on the menu that I didn't think they
could spoil. I ordered it and she brought it quickly. They
hadn't spoiled it, but they'd come close.

She brought my coffee, and said, "You been in here before,
I guess. I figured you looked familiar, kind of."

Far be it from me to tell her she'd seen me in the paper.
"I've been in before. Have you been here long?"

"A lifetime, mister."

"If you want to get off your feet, why don't you bring
some coffee and sit down and keep me company."

She glanced at the other booth with the two waitresses in
it. She looked with feral quickness and intentness toward the
counter. She said, barely moving her lips, "In a minute. The
boss is out back. He takes off soon now. When I see his car go
down the drive, I can. But until he goes, it could get me in
trouble."

She went back to the other booth. I heard them whisper-
ing over there. I heard some giggles. One girl went elabo-
rately over to the counter for nothing at all. She straightened
a metal napkin dispenser, turned around and studied me in-
tently as she walked back to the booth. I listened for the

gasps, but I just heard more giggling. They hadn't recognized me yet.

Just as I finished my meal, a car went down the driveway. One of the girls said, quite audibly, "Good night, Frankie, you big bastard. Sweet dreams."

The blonde brought coffee over and sat across from me and looked arch. "I'm Cindy."

"I'm Andy."

"Hi, Andy."

"Hi, Cindy." A sparkling routine.

"Jeez, my feet. He keeps yakking about a new kinda floor. But nothing ever changes in this joint. The floor is like rocks. You ought to walk on it all day."

"I guess it's worth it, though, isn't it? The tips and all."

Her laugh was a startling explosive bray, which she rendered without changing expression. "Tips? Here? Man, what you take to have those big happy dreams?"

"I always have happy dreams. I dreamed I was going to eat here and have a date with Joy."

"I guess you don't know her so good, Andy. Maybe some people would say she's pretty. I guess maybe she is. But she don't date. She's colder than a witch's—oops, I don't know you that good. Yet." The last word was drawled, though the rest was from Hamtramck.

"Didn't she date anybody?"

"You know something, Andy, I never could figure that girl. We had this dishwasher, see? I mean a real moody guy. Bright, kind of, and a lot of the time you'd figure he was laughing at you. Funny to have a punk washing dishes laughing at you and you don't know why. This was better than six months ago, see? In March, I guess it was, and, oh God, are we busy. People waiting to eat in this dump, can you imagine? So she eats here twice. And without no permission or nothing, the second time she come here, she goes charging right out in the kitchen, and the manager finds her out there, nose to nose with that Ken, the dishwasher, and them talking in low nasty voices to each other. See, she must have known he was working here. He'd been on for a couple of months. Well, he tells her—the manager I mean—that she's got to get out of the kitchen, and she steps up and asks him for a job. We need girls and he takes her on, and honest to God, she was green as beans. She kept getting all fouled up and, see, we had to get her straightened out on orders and things, and everybody in here busy as a college girl in a—oops, I still don't know you good enough, Andy. Anyway, she catches on fast and she does her share of the dirty work, and pretty soon she's a good waitress. We couldn't figure out what it was with the two of them. He had an old beat-up car, and sometimes after work they'd go off in it. But always acting kind of sore at each other. We kind of hinted around, but she wouldn't say anything. We tried to get her off on dates, but, no sir, not Joy. We're closed on Tuesdays here, and one Tuesday I even get the guy, this Ken, see, to take me out. I figured I could find out from him whether they were married, those two, or something like that, and he run out on her and she found him again, and took the job so she could be close enough to needle him or something. Anyway, he picks me up in that beat car. I live just down the road in that Glory-Bee Court, Gawd what a foul dump, but it's handy being so close by, and we're going swimming, see? I don't really like the guy. He gives me the creeps. He really does. I find out he doesn't want nothing to do with any public beach. Not him. Not good enough for him, I guess. On the way he keeps talking over my head. Smart stuff. Confusing me and making me sore. He goes over there where the big houses are, over there where it's all private beach, and there's one of those big houses empty, and he goes right in the driveway and parks, bold as anything, and he tells me he always swims there, and if somebody moves in, he'll find another empty house and do the same thing. He has busted the door of the cabana on the beach, and we change in there, but he doesn't get fresh or anything, like I thought maybe he would, and wished he would because, see, I had a big yen to smack him down good for all the wise talk. Well, he gets his swimming pants on and I see right off he's a real well-built guy, which I figured he was anyway, and he goes strutting down the beach and we spread the blanket and open some beer and he waves at people. I ask him how he knows them. He says he tells them he's the owner's friend, and if you do things bold, nobody stops you. It certainly made me nervous, and I kept wondering if the cops found us if I'd be in trouble too on account of busting into that cabana. He says he's making a lot of friends around there and he said if they knew what his line of work was, they'd drop their teeth. We swam and I'm a no-good swimmer, believe me, and boys usually help me in the water, but that lunk just swam out about forty miles and left me splashing around alone for a hell of a long time. When he comes back and we're drinking beer I try to wiggle some info out of him about Joy. But he's like clams, see. And like he's laughing at me. It got me sore. I drank a terrible big amount of beer, especially when he was way down the beach talking to people and he wouldn't let me come, like he was ashamed of me or something, and him only a dishwasher, the nerve! When I drink beer I always get terrible sleepy, so don't you feed me beer tonight, sugar, because I go out like lights. I can leave here pretty soon now and there's a real cute place about a mile down the road. It's just juke for dancing, but Gawd, I'd dance to a guy playing a paper comb if it come to that and there was nothing else. But to get back to that Ken—oh, Jeez, how he griped me. I go to sleep right there on the blanket and the funniest damn thing, I get a bad dream about drowning in the water, and I open my eyes and there are his eyes looking right down into mine, and at first I think maybe it is a pass and I get a chance to slap him down like I wanted to because he talked so wise to me, see, like I was ignorant or something, but it isn't that. It isn't no pass, Andy. It's just the fingers on my throat and him looking down at me. Gawd, have I had dreams about that! I didn't even dare twitch. Him looking at me like he was one of those professors looking down at a bug and wondering where to stick the pin through, I tell you, I was all through, right there. Then all of a sudden he takes his hand away and gives a little shrug like I wasn't worth sticking a pin through, like I was a dull kind of bug not worth collecting. He says we better go and I say we better had, and I feel a lot better when he's ten feet away, believe me. Still there's no pass, and he brings me back and he doesn't even want to come in for a drink. Well, it was maybe—let me see—May? Early in May, I guess, he quits. No notice—no nothing. Frankie popped a couple guts, believe you me. Joy gets awful quiet-like, but she keeps on working. We figured he blew town. Then a good customer of mine who knows him by sight tells about seeing him driving one of those new little foreign-type cars. So you know how I got it figured out? She worked here until she could get a better job because she knew he was still in town, see. And I bet he got himself some rich babe he met on that beach, and she's keeping him because, like I said, he's a pretty well-built fella, and that would be just his style. He always acted like he was too good for dishwashing. And a guy like that, I mean a guy who'll bust into places like that, he just doesn't give a damn. My God, the coffee is terrible tonight. Honey, let's you drive me to my place and I'll change and I got a bottle there, and then we can go dancing. It isn't air conditioned there but it's cool."

"What was Ken's last name?"

"God knows. I don't even think Frankie knew. He just walked in one day when Frankie had a sign in the window about a dishwasher, and he was always going to get his social security number looked up or something, and he never did, even though Frankie kept after him."

"Where did he live when he worked here?"

"Down the line some place. Somebody said, I forget who, that he was in a shack on one of the islands in the bay. Some little island where you got to wade across the flats to get to it, and I guess that's right because he was always coming in with his shoes soaked in the morning. I bet you he's moved off that island now. I bet he's living up with some rich bag in one of those big houses. I don't know why a girl like Joy would want to toss herself away on a bum type like that. I can shove off now. Gee, maybe you don't like dancing. My place is sort of crumby, and all the movies stink. I looked them up. You know, Monday night is sort of like a weekend to me, the way we're closed Tuesdays. I mean I can sleep all day, and I usually do because I'm up all night. That is, if you don't feed me beer. Then I get awful dopey and I'm no good to anybody, but I bet you aren't the type of fella buys beer."

She stood up, and one of the other girls said, "Have a good time, honey."

I had been just about to apply the brush-off, but it suddenly seemed too bad to make that much of a dent in her pride. I decided, to save her face, that I'd leave with her and then apply the brush-off at her place.

I paid the check, and we went out and got in the car. The grease smell was caught in her hair. I could detect it when we were inside the car. I started up and swung out into the road and headed for Glory-Bee Court.

"What do you usually do Monday nights?"

"Oh, when I don't have a date—that doesn't happen often, see—well, I go on down to that cute place I was telling you about. There's a gang of nice kids goes there. We have a lot of laughs and play some table shuffleboard, and you ought to see Bernie the bartender do imitations. Honest to God, his Charles Boyer is a riot."

I turned into the floodlit driveway of Glory-Bee. "The one on the end. It's more private-like. Of course when the season starts, I got to move back into town because the prices go way up in the courts. What's this? Pictures, hey."

I tried to snatch them but I was too late. She had the top picture turned toward the floodlights. She slid them slowly back into the envelope. She turned slowly to face me as she placed the envelope between us. Her voice was entirely different. "Where's your camera, you bum?"

"What do you mean?"

"I know about guys like you. I know the racket. Please, baby, just one little picture. Just a keepsake. Then you bastards make a million prints and sell them all over the country. I had a girl friend in Detroit who got sucked into that one.

She was so dumb she let this guy take some special movies of her. Then her husband's old man goes to a smoker and sees her in the movies. Why don't you guys hire tramps? You're just too damn cheap, I guess. You don't sucker me, mister. I'm just not that damn dumb. I've been around a couple of years. We would have had a good time tonight until you pulled out a camera, buster, and then I'd have screamed your damn ears off, so maybe you're lucky, after all. I should hope to drop dead if I'd walk ten feet with you in the sunshine on a busy street. You stink."

She half ran to her door. I turned around and got out of there. My ears were burning. I felt ashamed—I guess merely because I was a member of the same race that had developed that kind of racket. She had been almost pathetically vulnerable. So arch and coy once she thought she had a date. I knew I'd never dare go back there.

Anyway, she had helped—a lot. I could drop that name I'd used for him—Joe. Now it was Ken. And in a lot clearer focus. Mary Eleanor on the beach. And that "well-built fella" moving in on her. A lot easier than breaking into a cabana. This was like breaking into something where the door wasn't even locked.

So they'd gone to Miami together. At least it was probable that they had. But he would have come back with her. I wondered why the pictures had been mailed from Miami. That didn't make much sense. Unless Ken, too, was a dupe, and they had stayed together at the wrong place, and he received no part of the forty thousand. I was so fond of my structure that I had built up that I resented any little fact which didn't fit into it perfectly. But the picture of Ken was becoming distressingly clear. And I had to give up the idea of a rational being with larceny and murder in his heart. Cindy's picture of Ken set it up as a distorted intelligence, perhaps over-endowment and overtones of the psychopathic. And that made what had happened to Christy fit better. Killing her had seemed needless, from any rational point of view. But if the need were in the mind of the killer . . . Perhaps Wargler and I were both right. It was related to John's death, and un-related at the same time. Two opposing facets of irrational-ity. A headless man standing death-quiet in the brush of Tickler Terrace. I was sorry about Cindy. There was more to ask her.

Fifteen

IT WAS ELEVEN-THIRTY when I parked, once again, in the dark driveway in front of the Long house, and heard the Gulf as I turned off the motor. If the burly young policeman was still staked out there, I was going to make him let me talk to Mary Eleanor, even if I had to phone Wargler and get him over here, phone Steve and get him here, too, get Jack Ryer— open the whole thing up and let them take over. Maybe one quick look at the photographs, and the young cop would see that there was something to be discussed. I could bluntly and directly ask Mary Eleanor where Ken was. Maybe we'd have to walk her around and give her a cold shower and put hot coffee into her, but it ought to bring her back out of green dragon land soon enough.

I pushed the bell. I knocked softly, and then when there was no answer, I knocked loudly. I yelled into the darkness of the house: "Hey! Hey, in there."

Maybe they'd moved faster than I had. Maybe, once again, I'd underestimated the fat sleepy chief, and Cro-Magnon George. They'd all be back in town, and the house would be empty. I could see a dim light shining from her bedroom door into the hallway. I tried the screen and the latch was still broken, and the cylinder overhead made a soft sighing sound as I pushed it open, made a Japanese apology as it shut behind me.

I went down the hall walking loudly, setting my feet down firmly, as I did not want the policeman to shoot.

I walked into the room saying, cheerfully, as insurance, "It's only me again."

There was a bed lamp on. It had a small blue shade, quite heavy, so that most of the light was directed downward. But enough of it slanted out across the floor so that I was able to avoid setting my foot on the face of the young policeman. He lay there the way a child sleeps, ruddy cheek against her rug, left hand near his face, palm up, fingers slightly curled. On the right side of his head, over the ear and just behind the temple, was a comedy touch—a half a hen's egg that had to be makeup. Nobody could swell up like that. His cap was a couple of feet from his head. His breathing was shallow and fast. You see a big man like that, you inevitably think of how he was as a little kid. Ralphie banged his head falling out of that nasty old tree, and Mother put witch hazel on it and tucked him in and kissed his cheek, which tasted of salt from too many tears. The light struck him in such a way that I saw he had very long eyelashes, something you would never notice under other circumstances.

In the dark house the phone began to ring. It had the sound of all phones in empty houses. Nobody here, boss.

Nobody here but us chickens. I mechanically counted the rings. Six, seven, eight, nine, ten—and half of eleven. Then just the Gulf sound, the quick shallow breathing.

She still wore the flimsy robe. She had rolled onto her back and the robe was parted, and she was a deep oven brown except for the narrow glaring white band across her loins. And deep brown except for her throat. I stood by the bed. The weapon used had been placed, after use, on her flat brown belly. It was a most casual, arrogant touch. The weapon was a pair of small curved nail scissors. From the look of her throat it had not been the handiest weapon in the world. It had taken a bit of prying and prodding to find and open the jugular. The hard spurt of blood had gouted upward at a slant, darkening her left cheek, matting her dark hair to the pillow on the left side, impacting viscidly against the wall beyond the head of the bed. Slack lips had slid back from the oversized teeth. There had been a great deal of blood, an incredible amount. It was drying, and it had a hot sick odor. Under the brown skin of her face was the skull shape, accentuated by the slant of lamplight.

I was tired of looking at the face of death.

I was tired of the thought of death, tired of delicate machines interrupted in their course. Life had burst out through the throat of both the Longs, and left them shrunken.

The phone began again. I counted the rings as I went out and searched for it, found it on a low table near the glass window wall. There was phosphorescence in the Gulf waves, a billion tiny creatures were twinkling and dying.

"I am certainly *glad* to get *somebody* on this line! Who is this speaking! I *must* speak to Mrs. Long. This is William Dangerfield, and I *certainly* want *some* expression of opinion on what sort of ceremony she wants for the deceased tomorrow."

My brain felt like an ancient reluctant engine. That starter was turning it over slowly, but it wouldn't catch. "What?"

"*Please*, whoever you are. My goodness, if she can't come to the phone, for heaven's sake talk to her and find out what she wants. *Nobody* has even selected a *casket* for the deceased. And how in the world can I arrange a permit when *nobody* has told me where the deceased is to be buried? I'm *frantic*, I tell you."

"Mrs. Long is also deceased," I said woodenly.

"What? What! What was that?"

"Mrs. Long is dead, too. Just like her husband. *D-e-a-d*."

The voice lost its urgency. It seemed to collapse in upon itself. "I'll be a son-of-a-bitch," it said in lost, tired resignation. There was a click and he was gone.

I went back to the bedroom. The policeman had rolled onto his back. He breathed through his open mouth and his fingers made motions as if he were feeling the texture of the rug. His eyes opened and he looked blankly up at the ceiling. I stood over him and his eyes slowly changed direction, stared stupidly at me. He grunted then and his eyes narrowed, and he sat up with a great gasp and skittered backward on his fanny and grabbed at the gun in the holster and got it out, and there was only a blind instinct in his eyes. I made a dive toward him and pushed the gun away and he fired twice, as I lay half sprawled across his legs.

"No!" I yelled. "No!" And my ears were ringing with the hard impact of the shots in the quiet of the room.

He seemed to have needed the sound of the shots to bring

him back to here and now. The tension went out of him and
I cautiously drew back and knelt by him, my eye still on the
revolver. He turned the gun wrist up and stared at his watch.

"Oh, dear God," he said weakly.

I got up and extended a hand to help him up. He waved
the gun at me. "Stand over against the wall," he said. I did.
He shook his head gingerly, reached around with his left
hand, and tenderly touched the lump. He winced, grunted
up onto his feet, and weaved a bit, squeezing his eyes tightly
shut for a moment.

Keeping the gun aimed in my general direction, he half
turned and looked at what was on the bed.

"Oh, dear God," he said again in the same tone. He looked
at me and he pouted as though he were close to tears. "Goddamn you, McClintock, if you did this—"

"When did it happen?"

"I got banged on the head about ten-thirty."

"At ten-thirty I was sitting in a restaurant at least four
miles from here, and I've got at least five witnesses to that. I
got here ten minutes ago."

He staggered a little and moved over to a flimsy-looking
chair and sat down heavily. He looked at me, looked at the
gun in his hand, shoved it back in the holster. He put his elbows on his knees and his face in his hands and shuddered. "I
feel terrible," he said.

"What happened?"

His voice was muffled by his hands. "I'm waiting and I
don't hear a thing. All of a sudden somebody starts whisper-
ing. 'Come here, please. Come here, please.' Like that. I
thought it was her. I thought she woke up and maybe she was

sick. So I come out and stand by the bed. Then I hear her snoring and I tried to turn fast but—I never did get all the way around. Suckered—that's what I was! Somebody whispers, you can't tell if it's a man or a woman."

He lifted his head and sighed and got up and went over to the bed and looked down at her. "Oh, brother!" he said in an awed voice. He took a step back and turned and I saw his throat work as he swallowed a few times, quickly. He rubbed his hands across his mouth, and said, "I better call in. God, how am I going to tell them about it?"

I waited in the room, listening to his low voice on the phone. I looked around to see where the bullets hit. I turned on another light and found them, at least found the holes splintered into the paneling three feet off the floor and about two feet apart. For the unconscious man, there had been no awareness of the passing time. When he had awakened he had evidently thought I was the person who had just a few moments before knocked him down.

He came back in and sat down again. "What a head," he mumbled. There was a curious gargling sound from the object on the bed, a sound that prickled the hair on the back of my neck and the skin on the backs of my hands, and turned me rigid.

He stood mildly at the bed. "Gas," he said. "Gas in the gut. Deads'll do that. I heard it a couple times in Korea."

There was a thin sound in the night. We listened. Sirens coming fast. He stood up heavily. His color wasn't good. He half turned toward me and there was an odd expression on his face, like a half-smile of apology. Then his eyes rolled upward and his knees gave way, and he went down before I could get to him, went down with a thud which shook the house and rattled the bottles on the glass top of Mary Eleanor's dressing table.

It was quarter after two before people finally stopped yelling in my face and waving their arms at me and interrupting every time I tried to tell them something. Wargler himself, with George along, had taken me out to Glory-Bee, and then down the highway until we found the "cute" dive and found Cindy drinking beer at the bar. The four of us gathered in a little back room.

"Say, I'm glad you nailed this dirty son-of-a—"

Wargler looked pained. "Don't use bad words, you. Were you with this guy at ten-thirty?"

"Yes, I was that stupid. But when I found out, I didn't stay with him, see. I'm not that type girl, see."

"What type?"

"To pose for his dirty pictures. What else? You arrested him for it, didn't you?"

It had got me placed at ten-thirty, but it brought up a new topic to yell at me about. The trouble was, I couldn't remember where I'd left the pictures. Somewhere in Mary Eleanor's house, I thought. We roared back there at one-thirty, and there was a man posted and the body had been taken away and Jimmy was still taking pictures and prints. The familiar envelope was on the phone table. Wargler turned on a big aluminum floor lamp and sat down and took out the pictures. George looked over his shoulder.

"Good God Almighty!" Wargler said, almost with a tone of reverence. "Where'd you get these nasty things?"

"Look, here's the story. Apparently John found them. They—"

"Answer the question. Where'd *you* get them?"

"Out of the bottom of the Kenney girl's bureau."

"Where did *she* get them?"

"I think she got them out of John Long's desk. I think she broke into the desk and got them."

"O.K., how did you know there were any such pictures?"

"I didn't. Mary Eleanor told me to look for the envelope."

"Want to try proving that?"

"You know damn well I can't prove it!"

"Stop that damn bellering."

"If you'd only listen to me. If you'd only let me talk for ten minutes without asking a bunch of idiotic questions, maybe you'd learn—"

"Shut up!"

And that's the way things went until quarter after two. Every time I had to walk, George would push me just often enough in the back to keep me off balance. At a quarter after two I got smart. The Chief's office was crowded, and everybody looked stained, strained and weary. Jack, Steve, the Chief, George, Jimmy, and a couple of policemen whose names I didn't know, one of whom was taking notes.

"How come she wanted *you* to get those pictures?" Wargler demanded.

"I'm not answering another damn stupid question."

"You can't do that to me," Wargler said. "Your lawyer is right here. You heard him tell you to answer questions."

"I won't answer any more, because you never give me a chance to tell you what's important. If you'll close that big mouth for ten minutes, and if nobody interrupts me, I'll try to give you the whole thing. But if there's one question asked, one interruption, you can all go to hell in a bucket."

"Who do you think is giving the orders around here?"

Jack Ryer said easily, "Why don't you give it a try, Chief? It won't hurt anything."

I tried to look calm. Finally Wargler nodded, saying, "Go ahead."

I tried to tell it like a story. I started with Ken getting a job as a dishwasher. I guess I did it right, because before I'd said fifty words they had all got silent and rigid. There was no sound in the crowded office except my voice and the intermittent rustle as the sweating cop-secretary filled one sheet and whipped over to the next one.

"And finally," I said, "knowing that I was free, knowing that his biggest source of danger was Mary Eleanor Long, knowing that he had to shut her up permanently, he had to risk it. He came and killed her. John Long can't talk. Christy can't talk. Mary Eleanor can't talk. He's gone the full circle. Maybe he's in that shack on the island. I don't know. I don't know where the island is, or even if that Cindy was right."

There was a long silence. Wargler said petulantly, "Why the hell didn't you tell us all this quicker?"

He saw the expression on my face and looked away uneasily and rattled his ridged fingernails on the desk top. "Jimmy, go get them air pictures out of the files."

Jimmy came back in five minutes with a sheaf of big clear pictures of the bays, taken from the air. Wargler spread them out on his desk. Jack Ryer moved around to stand behind him, peering over his shoulder.

Jack said, "I do enough bay fishing, so I can tell you which ones you can wade to. This one here—and here. This set of three in a row over here. Then here's three, four, five down below Shay's Pass."

"Ten of 'em," Wargler said. "George, you do bay fishing, too. Which ones have shacks on 'em?" George pointed silently to three. "That all?" George nodded.

Jack said, "An old duck lives in the shack on that island. That leaves us these two."

Wargler said, "Well, eliminate that one because the guy is supposed to have a car, and it would be a two-mile walk through swamps to get to that one. If you fellas know what you're talking about, then he lived or is living on this one here."

I stood by the desk. You could see a roof, a small roof, through the trees. The island was the shape of a lima bean and seemed to be about a hundred yards long. The deep water passes showed up clearly, and it was plain that only about sixty feet of flats separated the island from the mainland. On the mainland you could see the curve of a secondary road that came to within fifty feet of the bay front. But the bay front there was such a low tangle of mangrove that it hadn't yet been cleared, filled, and built on.

Wargler said, "The sucker, if he's there, might have a boat. You can't tell. We got to coordinate this. George, you go call Odum Davis and tell him to get on down to his boat and get it ready to roll. George, you and Al go with Odum. And you can go along with them if you want to, Jack. Let's take a look at the time. We ought to fix it to get there at, lemme see, quarter to four sharp. We'll cut off the road side, and if he's on there, you bring him back in the boat, George. No damn need wading around in the dark getting hit with a stingaree. If he makes a run, provided he's there, we nail him ashore. Jimmy, lock up this McClintock."

"No, dammit!" I said. "Who has been steering you onto

him? I wanted to get him myself for—for personal reasons. Now he's yours, but you ought to be fair enough to at least let me go along."

"Withholding evidence," Wargler said. "Barging around messing things up like one of those private eyes in the books. God, if I ever hear one of the operatives called a private eye any place but in a book. McClintock, you've been a goddamn nuisance. But, O.K. Come on. You come with me."

The details were set up. We took two cars. We started fifteen minutes after Odum had cast off, starting chugging down the channel.

There was no moon. The town was flat on its back and snoring as we went through. I sat in the back in the first car, beside Jimmy. Steve was in front with the Chief.

Sixteen

ALL THE WAY OUT THERE I thought of Christy, and I felt alone. Even in the car with the three of them, with Wargler's big shoulders hulking against the headlight gleam on the road ahead, with Steve's cigar smoke being whipped back on the warm night air, I felt alone, as though Christy and I had been the only two live people in the world, and all these others were cleverly animated puppets, their bellies full of straw, clockwork brains.

Wargler slowed. "This here is the turn." He pulled over onto the shoulder and we got out.

"Here's the car, Chief!" Jimmy said, suppressed excitement in his voice. We went over to it. It was nosed down the slope of the shoulder, the hood under the dark trees. Wargler put his light on it. It was old, dusty, beat up, and gray. Wargler went down onto one knee and held the back of his hand against the tail pipe. He grunted.

"Warm?" Jimmy asked.

"No. But it's a long time since that woman got herself killed." He turned the light on his watch. "Three-forty. Should be a path here."

There was—a narrow path that was dry at first and then turned mushy underfoot as we neared the water. Mosquitoes fell on us with shrill cries of delight, yelling to all their relatives to pile on and have some nice blood. We cursed softly and slapped and lighted cigarettes. Finally we came to the edge of the water, humpy with mangrove roots and smelling of low tide.

Wargler started out across the water, peering into the faint starlight. Mullets thrashed and splashed off to our left. "There he is," Wargler said. "Moving in close."

I could barely make out the blob that was a boat. There was a splash and then another, and a flick of flashlights.

"Wading ashore," Wargler said. "Shallows off too slow to bring her right in."

We could see the intermittent lights once they got into the trees. We waited and slapped and scratched and blew smoke and waved our arms. They were nailing me through the back of my shirt. I wanted one small satisfaction—a minor one. A chance to just edge close enough to him, if he was there, and smash my fist into his mouth. Just leave one mark on him.

We couldn't see the lights any more. Then somebody lit a gasoline lantern, and it shone hard blue white through the oblong of a window.

Jack yelled, "Chief! Hey, Chief!"

"Anybody there?"

"Yes, he was here. He was sleeping. He says his name is Ken. We're bringing him along. No fuss."

"Good. We're going. About to get eat alive here."

We hurried back through the woods and piled into the cars with sighs of relief and got out of there. If you saw even the first rocket take-off to Mars, you'd pay little attention to it if you had to stand in a cloud of mosquitoes to watch it.

Once the wind had blown the car clean of the little black demons, I could start thinking about Ken again. It seemed almost too easy. There should have been a running gun fight, wild yells in the night. Too quiet, just waking up a man and taking him in.

It was a half-hour before the car drove up in front and they brought him inside to the Chief's office. When I heard his footsteps coming down the hall, then heard somebody say, "Right in here," I found out that up until that minute I had never known what hate was. The thing I used to call hate was just cold anger. This was something else. This was like a sickness. This was like getting hit in the belly.

He came in quietly. And he was the man I had seen that night through the office window, just as I had thought he would be.

He wore a clean white shirt and faded khaki pants, wet halfway to the knees from wading out to the boat. He had a perfectly acceptable face. All the features in the right places. His eyes were gray and his mouth was firm. His brows were sufficiently arched to give him a faint look of surprise. His brown hair was cropped short, and he leaned over after he sat down and carefully put a sand-colored snap-brim fabric hat under the chair where the braces crossed.

He was almost a normal-looking guy. But he brought something strange into the now-familiar office. I know I felt it. And, glancing at Jack Ryer's faintly puzzled face, I know he must have felt much the same thing.

He gave me the feeling that I was carrying excess baggage— that I was burdened down with self-doubt, and moral conjectures and vague fragments of philosophies. He made me feel that my normal soul-confusion, all the inward turmoil of merely being a human being, was actually a bit silly—a lessening of efficiency. He was not burdened thusly. He looked as specialized as a knife blade. He brought something chilly and alien into the office, something you felt instinctively, something he compounded by a stillness which at first I did not understand. It took a moment to see that it was a complete lack of mannerisms, of any of the useless movements we indulge in.

Ken merely sat—and looked. And his feet rested flat on the floor and his hands rested on his thighs. He breathed and sat and looked.

That strangeness was in the air, like the echo after a gong has been struck. Men are going to feel that way when the first visitor from outer space sits among them. Kids could feel that way if a man with a battle ax suddenly appeared in the middle of a pillow fight. We were all soft in our special ways, and formless in our individual ways, and this man-thing was silent, and it sat, and you knew that it was amused. The man-thing turned its head slowly and looked at me. I knew then what Cindy meant. I was a bug, but not of sufficient interest to warrant collection.

Wargler looked uncertain. He slid the pictures out of the envelope, all fourteen of them. He had previously got hold of Steve and had him bring his seven in, to add them to mine.

Wargler looked at the pictures in silence. He selected one, came around the desk, snatched Ken's wrist, looked at the watch. There was no resistance, no change of expression. Wargler had immediately selected the most immediate method of identification. He released the wrist. Ken left his arm poised there for a moment, returned it slowly to his lap.

Wargler held the picture inches in front of Ken's nose, and said, "Do you deny this is you?"

Ken frowned with regal annoyance and gently pushed Wargler's heavy hand a bit farther away. He looked at the picture. "Wouldn't it be just a shade pointless to deny that? A bit self-evident, isn't it?" His voice was soft and deep, and he enunciated carefully.

"Then you admit it?"

"You seem to infer a broader admission than you have stated. Wouldn't it be more intelligent to state whatever it is that I am expected to admit?"

"I'll do this my way!"

"Obviously."

Wargler went around the desk and sat down. "All right. Do you admit that you had these pictures taken so you could use 'em to blackmail Mrs. Long?"

"No. I shouldn't care to admit that."

"The truth, isn't it?"

"The truth is that Mary Eleanor is—shall we say, sentimental in her own rather unique way. She wanted some—rather vivid memento of our little moments of sensual pleasure. I see they have been rather spoiled—cut up like that. I am quite sure that should you take the trouble to inquire of her, she will admit that she dotes on such—souvenirs.

As a matter of fact, she forced me to go to quite a bit of trouble in Miami to arrange to have those taken. She's rather a silly little person, you know. Very animalistic."

"You know damn well she's dead. You know damn well we can't ask her anything because you killed her and put Tom Garver in the hospital with a concussion."

"Is she dead?" he asked politely. "That seems rather a waste, doesn't it."

"You cold-hearted bastard!" Wargler said.

Ken's eyes didn't even flicker. "She was hardly more than an acquaintance. Sorry I can't be more concerned. And I'm afraid I don't know anyone named Garver."

"You killed her husband and you killed her."

"I'm sorry. You must be mistaken. I permitted some rather—shall we say, unflattering pictures to be taken. If there's some statute against that, I shall be glad to—pay any penalty you see fit to impose."

"Out of the forty thousand bucks that you pried out of her?"

"Oh, *come* now! Really! If I had that much money, I believe I would have invested in some creature comforts. That's an excessively dank little island."

"Why did you kill John Long?"

"Now I am afraid I am going to have to tell you something which might make you quite annoyed with me. During the evening before Mr. Long was killed, Mary Eleanor drove out to visit me. She called and I waded ashore. She seemed nervous and upset. Her husband had found her little souvenirs you have there some time before that—several weeks before that. She seemed desperately afraid of him. I believe it was about two o'clock in the morning. She said she was going to do something. She didn't care to tell me what. I walked her to her little car, and she had an object in the seat beside her. One of those underwater arrangements where the propelling force is heavy rubber, in strands. She was very upset, I repeat. And she said she had an appointment, so she drove off. You understand, I was becoming quite weary of her. She is—I guess past tense is more accurate—was, except for what I shall politely term her hobby, quite a desolate little bore. Absolutely no conversation. I met her on the beach, you know. When I heard of the murder the next day, I was quite naturally upset."

"I can imagine!" Wargler said heavily.

"There's no need to take that tone. I was upset, not for her, but as to whether I should come in and give you my information. Then when I read of the arrest of—Mr. McClintock, is it?—I thought I had let my imagination run away with me. I can see now, of course, that I should have come in with my information."

Wargler bit his lip. He suddenly shifted his approach. "Did you work as a dishwasher out at Frankie's Kitchen?"

"Yes, I did. A very poor restaurant, by the way."

"Aren't you a pretty well-educated fella to wash dishes for a living?"

"I'm sufficiently well-educated, sir, to know that it is a much more rewarding profession, from the viewpoint of keeping one's soul intact than—for example—police work. I hope you can follow me."

Wargler looked like a man who had just found a hair in the tapioca pudding. "Why did you quit?"

"I'm afraid that, too, is rather self-evident. I became a pro-tégé. Mrs. Long was quite generous. I suppose it was in payment for services rendered. My wants are simple and except for our trips, I do not feel I was any great drain on her resources. Perhaps not as much as she—as she was on mine." For the first time he smiled slightly.

"A damn gigolo, eh?" Wargler asked.

"I'm afraid so. And not quite as clean a line of work as washing dishes, I assure you. Though I am perhaps more indifferent than most people to the moralistic aspects of whatever I choose to do."

"While you worked as a dishwasher were you acquainted with a young woman named Joy Kenney?"

"While I worked there? Don't you think—I mean, if this is considered to be an informal interrogation, don't you think you should ask me my full name?"

Wargler turned deep red. "What's your name?"

"Roy Randolph Kenney."

I heard a few suppressed gasps. And I knew at once what it was that had rung the distant bells in the back of my mind. Arch of brows, firmness of mouth.

"Your wife!" Wargler barked.

"His sister," I said involuntarily. Wargler gave me a quick glance of annoyance.

"Is that right?" he asked Roy Kenney.

"Roy and Joy. Rather quaint, don't you think? My sibling. With a rather pronounced—almost psychopathically strong—maternal urge. My nemesis, gentlemen."

"That why she went to work out there, too?"

"Isn't that obvious? Joy seems to feel that my adjustment to the world I seem to be condemned to live in, is not of the best. I'm a bit of a wanderer. Joy always finds me, somehow. She's got enormously clever at it. I was really quite shocked when she walked in, because I thought this time I had completely escaped. It turned out to have been quite easy for her. She had written to motor vehicle bureaus in the South, as she knows I prefer warm climates. When I began work in Florida, I had to acquire a Florida title to my car and give up the Mississippi plates. Tallahassee gave her my address. I had used the restaurant as an address. She's a good, earnest, dedicated child. To my dismay, I seem to be the outlet for her dedication."

"Why does she follow you around?" Wargler asked. "You keep getting in trouble?"

"Trouble? No, rather I believe that it is because she seems to feel that I am—shall we say, wasting myself, and my poor talents. She has the rather strange impression that should I settle down, I could acquire vast amounts of worldly goods. She can't quite understand that I am perfectly contented to wander, to work when it seems important, to live as well as I can with a minimum of exertion and responsibility. I believe she will confirm that for you."

"She can't confirm anything," Wargler said.

Roy Kenney leaned forward a few inches. I had the sudden feeling that what I had thought was a steel blade was merely a shining scabbard. And now, suddenly, the actual blade was drawn. "What do you mean, sir?" he asked.

"I mean that your sister has lost her marbles, Kenney. Doc Vayse says she's cata—cata—"

"Catatonic," Jack supplied.

"That's the word. Like a zombie. And don't kid me. The pair of you tried a big fancy shakedown, and then you got scared and started killing people and that's why she's off her rocker."

The blade was returned to the scabbard and Roy Kenney leaned back again. "I might suggest, sir, that as long as we seem to be discussing mental conditions, you might get a diagnosis of those delusions you seem to have. Frankly, they sound rather wild to me."

"I'm wild," Wargler said, "and I don't mean crazy. Why'd your sister angle a job in John Long's office?"

"She was distressed at my—liaison with Mrs. Long. She didn't wish to see her precious brother dismembered by a primitive and excitable husband. I am not quite clear about her motivation. Perhaps she hoped to keep an eye on Mr. Long and warn me in time. Or perhaps she was indirectly threatening me with exposure, so that I would give up Mrs. Long."

"How come she had these pictures?"

"Did she? That's a bit—distressing. Joy has no taste for the seamy side; it makes her quite ill. Perhaps, after Mr. Long died, she searched his possessions to make certain there was nothing there which might point to my—relationship with Mary Eleanor. Rather a fortunate thing that she did so, from my point of view, perhaps. But it all is rather confusing at this point. Joy will be all right, I am certain. She is a bit— unstable at times. But she comes out of it. And comes out of it rather rededicated to saving me. It is almost a religious fervor. Take care of your brother. It was, in fact, a deathbed request, so I shouldn't resent it so much, perhaps. But it does get a bit sticky having a protective sister hanging about your neck like an albatross."

"You're older than she is," Wargler said. "How come she has to promise to look after you? I'd think it would be the other way around?"

"During her—last years, my mother seemed to share my sister's concern about my economic and social future."

"Because you were always getting in trouble?"

"My dear sir. Please understand that both you and I are living in a world so regimented that having an outlook which can be called different is half-sin and half-crime. I live my way, and enjoy it. I do not require approval."

"O.K., Kenney. You're just different. You're so damn different you don't turn a hair about strangling a girl and tossing her in the bay, just because you figured she maybe found out too much from your sister."

Roy Kenney stared at him without change of expression. "Is this some entirely new murder? Of course. That girl in today's paper—Hallowell? I believe you are on the track of an entirely new police theory, sir. At least it is new to me. When you have a sufficient number of crimes of violence, pick up the nearest suspect, and twist facts until he can be made responsible for all of them. Really, don't you feel that this is becoming a bit absurd?"

"What do you think it was that your sister told Christine Hallowell about you? It must have been something important for you to go out there and kill her, and then go tell your sister you'd done it, and drive her mad."

"Listen in next week. Find out what it was that the fiend believed had been given away by little Joy. Find out why the fiend strangled Christine and Mary Eleanor. By the way, is that the way Mary Eleanor was killed, too? If so, I should think that you would look for someone who goes about strangling persons. I certainly don't. Except for my philosophical beliefs about the business of living, sir, I am a very ordinary man."

He could say it. He could sit there for a month and keep saying it and he would never sell any one of us in the room. He was no ordinary man. He was evil, sitting there and laughing inside, laughing fit to split. He was covered, all the way up and down the line, and he knew it. We knew we couldn't touch him.

"You deny that you threw Miss Hallowell in the creek out there to Shady Grove?"

"Of course."

Wargler leaned back and the chair creaked and he stuck his thumbs in his belt and he beamed at Roy Kenney. "Son, we're going to jail you."

"If your jail is comfortable, and it isn't more than a week or so, sir. But let's not carry all this too far."

"I think we're going to jail you for a few years, son. We've got a witness, haven't we, George?"

George nodded and got up and left the office, closing the door behind him.

Seventeen

THE SOUND OF George's heavy tromping faded quickly through the closed door. Wargler's chair creaked. He smiled at Roy Kenney.

At last Kenney said, "As I think about this, sir, I hope you will forgive my getting a bit worried. It occurs to me that with this much violence in a city of this size, there must be quite a bit of pressure on you. And I do not like the thought of becoming a sacrificial lamb—on faked evidence. I rather imagine your witness will be well trained."

"You don't have to worry, son. We don't work that way. Gawd damn it, I wisht that new tape had come in time."

"I'm getting everything, Chief," the policeman-stenographer said.

There was a long time of silence in the office. I looked around. Nobody except Wargler was looking directly at Roy Kenney. The rest of us kept our eyes away from him, as though it was a shameful thing such a person existed, and to look at him gave some confirmation of existence.

My mosquito bites were itching. Something had happened to the lights in the office. It took me a minute to figure it out. I looked then at the windows. It was early-morning gray out there. A gray world. The right time for snook in the pass. The time to get big reds near the jetties. The time when the Macks start to slash at the bait out in the Gulf.

What witness, I wondered? Elly had acted funny. I hoped to God she'd caught a glimpse of him. Anything to smash that smug exterior—anything to turn him into something that cringed.

It was funny how he could bring out the animal that crouches deep inside you all the time. We were a pack of tame dogs, forced to sit amicably with a wolf. But one little word and we'd fall on him and tear him to small bits.

The Chief started to hum "Humoresque" in the silence. "Dum deedum deedum dedum—dedum de dum de deedee dum—Hear 'em coming. Nervous, son?"

"Not very. Should I be?"

"That's up to your conscience. Would be, I mean, if you had one. I think you got a hole where it should have been."

They were at the door. We all looked at the door.

It opened and my throat filled and my eyes filled, and my fingers dug into my legs so hard I found the marks three days later and couldn't think for a time what had made them.

The door opened and my long-legged, brown-eyed blonde came in. My life came walking back through the door. My warm life stood there, just inside the door, and her eyes found mine first and they were filled with gladness. And I got to her, and the damn tears were running right down my face, and I manfully tried to suppress small broken-drain sounds, and got my arms around the good tall warm strong feel of her, with the sweet-scented hair, and her forehead grinding against my cheekbone in a well-remembered way, while all I could do was say her name, over and over, like an incantation.

We had blocked the door and George was still out there in the hall. There was an explosion of movement behind me and a hoarse yell, and before I could turn something drove hard into the small of my back. It was like being bunted by a city bus. It drove me right out the door, Christy in my arms, and we piled into George and all went down in a scrambling heap on the tile floor.

Somehow I landed across George, with Christy across me, pinning my legs. George reacted like a rodeo bull, bucking us both off his squat powerful frame. It slid me along on my face and I swung around in time to see George, on his stomach, rest the stubby barrel of a revolver on his forearm. The white shirt and khaki pants were running fleetly down the corridor which was dim with morning.

I saw George stick his tongue out of the corner of his mouth. The running figure was ten feet from the main door. George fired. The shot-sound was resonant in the corridor. The glass in the main door exploded and the tinkling sound as it broke on the tile was mingled with the sound of George's next shot. The door was swinging and I saw the khaki pants going down the steps, so just the white shirt was left. George fired the third time and the other half of the door exploded.

George sat up and looked about to cry. The whole herd

was thundering down toward the door. George grunted to his feet and ran heavily after them. They all went out into the gray morning, with the Chief yelling orders.

I helped my girl up. I kissed her. It was fine. I kissed her again. There were distant shots, and a yell, and more shots. I kissed my girl again. It was dizzy-making, so we leaned against the corridor wall. It was a serious and pleasant occupation.

We stopped when the Chief came back, mumbling and stamping his feet, hurrying along.

"Wait a minute," I said. "Hey! Chief!"

He went in and got on the phone. We heard him bellowing for the State Road Patrol. We went to the doorway. "Yeah. Headed south on the trail. Gray Chevy convertible. Yes, of course I got a car after him. Here's the plates."

I listened. "That's my car," I said weakly.

The Chief continued, "Roy Kenney. Five eleven. Hundred and seventy. Gray eyes, brown hair, white shirt, khaki pants. Unarmed. Wanted for murder, and you ask me, I think he's crazy."

He hung up and I glanced at Christy and went on into his office and said, with acute indignation, "Chief, just exactly what the hell was the idea in letting me think she was dead? Dammit, I ought to—"

"Shut up and go away. I got things on my mind."

"That's my car he's got."

"I know. After we picked you up I had Jimmy bring it around. He left it in front with the keys in it, damn him. And that George! George can't hardly hit the other end of the pistol range. Oh, dear God. Right out of my own office."

"Why did you let me think Christy was dead? Why?"

"Settle down, son."

Christy said, "You see, Andy, I saw him. I—I can explain it all, I think. Chief, could we go? Could we leave, please?"

"Sure. Just get out of the way."

I wanted to kick his fat head. Christy took my arm and tugged, and said, "Please, Andy."

I looked at her. It was too good a day to stay mad. It was the finest day I could remember.

We walked out. It was too early for a bus. I remembered that they had brought John's Cad in and put it in the lot beside the office. And I had his bunch of keys among the stuff returned to me. So we walked down arm in arm, unlocked his car, and got in. Before I started up, I turned to her, and said, "My God, you look good for a dead woman."

"You don't look so sharp, McClintock."

"I am pooped." I drove slowly, and said, "Talk!"

"Light talk? What would you like? Weather? Politics?"

I slowed down enough so I could turn and look into her eyes. "Some day, if there happens to be any words for it, and I think maybe they'll have to wump up a whole bunch of new words because the old ones won't half do, I'll tell you what happened to me when they told me—about you."

The sky was turning bloody in the east, and it was going to be a fine hot day. I turned into Tickler Terrace and let the car pussyfoot down the sand to my place. A slate heron stood on the bank of the creek, looking like ornamentation on a comic ashtray. His eyes, though, were as yellow and fierce as a hawk's. He half squatted and lunged up and pumped with his wings and suddenly he was something else entirely, something clean and free and not at all comic.

Christy held my hand in both of hers. She looked around and bit her lip. "It happened here, you know."

"From the beginning, hey."

"I found out where that girl lived, on Taylor Street, and I went to see her at four o'clock. It was a hard thing to do, Andy. There was no good place to start. She was hostile, you know. And nervous. And right from the start I knew that she knew something. And—Well, they had you locked up. I told her what it meant to me to have you accused of something I knew you didn't—couldn't do. And she wanted to know how I could be so sure you hadn't. That was pretty ridiculous, and it got me kind of sore. I accused her of protecting somebody. She sat on the bed and I sat on the chair, and she had such a lost look on her face.

"Finally she admitted she'd been protecting someone. She said she'd been protecting him for years. She said this person wasn't really bad. People didn't understand how it was with him. She said he sometimes did odd things, and he sometimes did—terrible things, but he wouldn't kill anybody. It wasn't in him to kill anybody. She said he'd been in trouble and he'd been in an institution, and if they found him, and if he was in any way implicated, they'd hold all those other things against him, and they wouldn't be fair to him. And that was why she had to protect him.

"We began to understand each other a little better then, Andy. I guess we both had—someone at stake. I was willing to use any weapon. You know. So I began to understand why she was so nervous and upset. And I looked at her and I said, 'Actually, though, you *are* terribly afraid that this time he has killed someone, and you don't know what to do about it.' She looked at me, and then, sitting there, she sort of toppled over on the bed and began to cry. I sat by her. It was pretty terrible. We found out we liked each other, and one of us had to lose.

"Anyway, she finally said it was something she would have to figure out for herself, and she wanted some time to think about it. She told me to come back later—quite a lot later. Then she would have a chance to make up her mind, and if she decided it was the right thing to do, we could both go down to the police station and she'd tell them the whole thing.

"I left and wandered around and went to a movie. Time went very slowly. Finally I went back there, quite late. She was entirely different. She was cool and very much in control of herself, and I could sense that she had seen the person she was talking about. She said that under no circumstances could she do anything so foolish as get that person mixed up in something, something where he hadn't done anything really wrong.

"I'd been so hopeful. It floored me. I didn't know what to do. I got a bus back out here, and I didn't know what to do next. I had tried to ask her about an envelope, like you said, but I didn't get anywhere."

Her hands tightened a bit on mine. "I was alone and I heard this funny noise, like someone scratching a fingernail on my screen door. You know how it is, being alone, and how little noises can get you. I went to the door and listened. Then I thought maybe it was some animal or something. I told myself not to be a darn woman, and I pushed the door open and stepped outside. He—he reached right out of the darkness and caught me by the throat and pulled me over into the shadows. His hand was like steel. I'm pretty strong and I tried to fight, and we sort of staggered over to where the light from the window was directly in his face. I've never seen a face like that—a look like that. I never want to see it again.

"He made funny little sounds and he said something about nobody going around knowing all about him. If he didn't have me by the throat maybe I could have told him she didn't tell me anything. But you know the way things go through your mind. I guessed she'd probably told him she *had* told me about him, to scare him or something. And then I remembered something my father told me a long time ago. Things were going around and around and the night seemed to be getting blacker. I just let myself go all limp. He lowered me to the ground and, like I hoped, let go of my throat. It was hard to get all the air I needed without making a gasping sound.

"He didn't move for a long time and neither did I. Then he bent over and picked me up. He carried me facedown across his shoulder, one arm around my legs. I let my arms hang limp, and his shoulder hurt my stomach. I'm heavy, I know, but it didn't seem to bother him. It's a terrible thing when you realize somebody wants to kill you. It's so—personal. At first you're just terribly frantic, and then you get kind of cold inside, like an animal or something, and you will do anything to keep it from happening.

"I guessed we were headed toward the bank of the creek. Even carrying me, he hardly made a sound. When we got to the bank, he just let go with his arm and sort of shrugged his shoulder to let me slip off. I fell right on that hard bank. He looked at the water and then he knelt down and put his ear against my chest. I knew I couldn't stop my heart beating, but I did stop breathing. He put his hand lightly on my throat, and then I guess he changed his mind. I guess he thought the water would do it. He took a handful of my hair and gave a terrible yank. I almost yelled, but I didn't. He stood up and kicked me, right here. God, you should see the bruise—in Technicolor. Then he took me by the hair and dragged me a little bit and gave one hard yank and let go, and I toppled right off the bank into the water. I got a real good lungful of air before I hit. I kept limp and let the current take me—sort of turning over and over. Right over there. That's where I went in. I had a chance to look at him once. He was a dark thing standing there watching me. Every time my face was out of the water, I took another deep breath. Finally I could hardly see the shore and I knew he couldn't see me, so I rolled onto my back and floated. Oh, those stars looked good! So good, Andy. The tide current took me down the bay a ways. I swam back to shore, and I came out down there in the mangroves, opposite where the gas station is. I didn't go to pieces until I got on dry land. Then it was terrible. I didn't dare come back here. I was just sopping. I didn't know what in the world to do. I knew I had to get in touch with the police. I went crawling up through all that underbrush and stuff until I got to the edge of the road. I kept back so headlights wouldn't shine on me. The gas station was closed. I went around to the back of it, and I picked up an empty oil can and broke the window. There wasn't any screen on the back window. I opened the catch and put the window up and pulled a crate over and climbed in. The phone is in front, and I was afraid headlights would shine in and somebody would see me, so I sat on the floor. It all took a lot longer than I thought. It was around three, I guess. I couldn't tell because

the water stopped my watch. I got Wargler on the phone fi-
nally and told him where I was. He came out with that
George, and I had climbed back out the window by then, and
I was waiting in the shadows.

"Wargler took me right to his house and his wife found a
robe that almost fit me after I took a shower to get the salt
off. Then I had a great big strong drink and we talked, and I
told them everything that had happened. The Chief decided
that I'd seen the man who murdered John Long, and if it was
announced that I was dead, it would give him a false sense of
security, so he'd stay around. Because if it came out that he
didn't . . . get me, then he might take off, knowing I could
identify him. He put a man to watch Joy's place and he said
they'd better not barge in and question her, because she might
alert the man, whoever he was. I asked if they could tell you
I was all right, and Wargler said he better not, and he said
he'd even give it out as a sex murder to make the man feel
even safer. He said you better not know, because he wanted
you to have the right reaction, and he didn't have much faith
in how well you could act. But he did promise he'd let you
out. I insisted on that, or I wouldn't stay hidden, I said. They
put me in the spare room, and I told the Chief what clothes
to bring out of my closet. And I asked him how they'd arrange it, and he said the Hoover brothers were his wife's first
cousins and they'd cooperate to make it look good, getting
my body in a net."

"That Wargler," I said wonderingly. "Had you like an ace
in the hole, and as soon as Roy Kenney saw you, he knew all
his time had run out, all at once. I can see what happened to
Joy now. From talking to her landlady, I knew he went back.
And I think he told her he'd killed you, and maybe told her

he'd kill anybody else she tried to talk to. And she could tell right then and there he'd gone over the edge, at last. Like when he killed the kitten in the barn, a long time ago. Then, there was her conflict. She *had* to turn him in. But emotionally she couldn't. She'd protected him for too long. So there was only one thing she could do. Retreat to some place where the decision wouldn't exist. She's basically, I guess, a good person. But there's some stain in that blood. He got more of it than she did. And she got just enough to live in her own type of hell. Anyway, if they can get back into that dark place where she's gone and get the information to her that the police know now, and that her brother is a fugitive . . . that ought to help bring her out of it because the conflict will no longer exist."

We got out of the car and walked, hand in hand, into my place.

I opened two cans of cold beer. She sat on my kitchen table and I leaned on the sink, and she made me go over everything that had happened. I'd been ramming around for nearly twenty-four hours, but looking at her was enough to make me feel like a good match for Marciano. The chill beer was nectar. Tickler Terrace was heaven.

It wasn't pleasant to tell about Mary Eleanor. It wasn't a happy thing to tell. Poor damn little wench, all fouled up inside, but not enough to get killed for it, not in that way, not with two keen little steel fangs twisting their way into the hollow at the base of the unconscious throat.

I covered all of it, for my Christy, and at the end my voice turned thick and rusty and my eyelids were packed with beach sand, and my leg bones were made from soft putty. The sun was up and I was looking at her. My eyes were focusing wrong. Her head would swell up to the size of a bushel basket and then fade away into something the size of a dime.

I looked at her and said, "A guy can be wrong, you know. He can underestimate something just because it comes with a few laughs. And never know it was exactly right for him until all of a sudden they take it away."

She looked shy. It looked right on her. Bridal and right.

"You would have found out," she said.

"At sixty-three. But you knew it, didn't you?"

"Of course."

"When?" I asked her.

"When does a thing like that creep up on you? Click, like a box top? Boing? Thud? Uh uh. Not like that. You realize it all of a sudden, but when you realize it you know you've had it coming on . . . like a virus."

"My goodness," I said, and I had to strain to focus my eyes to keep her from wavering.

She gave me a very fierce look. "Well?"

"What for you saying 'well'?"

"You're weaseling, McClintock. You're a-hemming and a-hawing all around barns and things. Do I live on inferences, yet? Or don't you think it would be manly? A girl has a right to hear the words. A girl likes the words. Get in the habit, McClintock, because I'm going to like to hear the words— forty times a day, eighty times a night. I've been waiting long enough. Come on."

I swallowed once and tried it for size. "I . . . uh . . . I love you."

"There, was that so hard?"

"Not as bad as I thought it would be. Here's one with a

little more confidence. I love you. And how about this one—I love you. My God, it gets easier, I love you."

She came over to me. "Hush, darlin'. This isn't a political rally. And I love you also, and have for some time, and will for some time into the future. Generations. Now come on, before you drop."

I suffered myself to be led into the bedroom. I sat on the edge of the bed, and she took off my shoes, and said, "This is once-in-a-lifetime service, I'll have you know."

"Uh," I said.

I went over backward like a collapsing tent. She swung my legs onto the bed. I felt the light touch of her lips on mine, and then on my forehead. Sleep grabbed me like a big black thing with teeth.

Eighteen

THEY LET ME SLEEP exactly one hour. Christy shook me awake. I felt as though my head were stuffed with wet cotton. I could make stupid gargling sounds and that was about all.

I sat on the edge of the bed, my head hanging on my spaghetti neck and became dimly aware that Elly and Ardy and some others of our Tickler Terrace group were crowded into my room. I raised my head. Ardy couldn't take his eyes off Christy.

"Please, Andy?" Christy said. "He's on the phone."

"Wha? Who?"

"Wargler. Right now."

The little group steered me down the road to Elly's house. I was a zombie. I grunted into the phone.

"McClintock? Damn you, it took you long enough."

"What is it? What do you want?"

"Are you drunk?"

"I'm just about to wake up."

"He didn't go far in that car of yours. He drove it about a mile south of where you are right now, and then ran it off the road down into the brush. George overshot it first, drove all the way to the road block and spotted it on the way back, so he's had over an hour to find a place to hide out. I'm getting dogs down there by the car, and I sent some people to get some of his clothes out of that shack for the dogs to start with. We tried to start your car. It's bound up tight. Won't turn over."

"I just had a new ring job on it," I said dismally.

"Then that did it. Look. Some of the boys will be out there to kind of keep an eye on you and the Hallowell girl. I think that maniac knows he's cooked and you can't trust 'em an inch. He'll want to finish what he started on that Hallowell girl, if he can get close enough. You understand what I'm saying?"

I turned and looked for Christy. She was talking to Ardy. I could see her standing out there in the sun. Out in the open.

"I understand."

"We're blocking the area good as we can. With every man and with volunteers. You stay close to that girl."

"O.K."

"He had an hour. I don't think he got another car. He's probably squatting in the mangrove someplace, waiting for dark."

He hung up. I went out into the sunlight. My watch said quarter of nine. Ardy looked like a man who had just broken the bank.

They all crowded around again, and I gave out the information. Everybody started eyeing the brush. Christy moved a little closer to me and bit her lip. As we were talking a police sedan swung in, let off a stranger and went back out again. This one had a face like one of the blue herons, with the same yellow fierce wild eyes.

He picked out Christy and me and herded us off, shooed the others away. Those who were late for work already took off for town. Elly resented being left out.

It was funny how the idea that he *might* be within fifty feet of us changed even the look of the sunshine. The water in the creek looked blacker. The whole world had a slightly alien tinge. Christy's fingers were like ice when I took her hand.

The new one was named Luffberry. He herded us into my place and then departed for a tour of the area. He came back and said, "I was supposed to look around and take you into town if I figured that would be better. The Chief's got it in his head Kenney might come here. He told me if I figured it was safe enough, we'd leave you here as a kind of a decoy, maybe. They's a man at that island, and one at the hospital, and one out to that restaurant, and one about every place he might head for. The roads are blocked and they's a couple little airplanes out looking for him in case he hits inland across country, or steals a boat and tries to go out in the Gulf. I guess we'll get him all right. Now you two stay in here and keep this place locked up and I'll be waiting over in your place, lady, in case he shows. Now if he comes here, you give a hoot and a holler and I'll be listening and come running. I'll tell all the other folks to stay inside their places, the ones what don't go to work."

He left us. I locked the doors. I found a place where she could sit and not be seen from the windows.

"Andy, you go to bed. I'll be all right."

"No thanks. Not while there's a chance of him showing up. I sat and watched him and listened to him talk. I respect him the way I respect the Red Army."

"I . . . saw him too. I'm all right."

"I'll wait with you."

"Andy, if he was going to come here, he would have, before they spotted his car. You need sleep, darling."

I prowled around. I unlocked the side door off the kitchen and looked cautiously into the garage, and then hustled out and grabbed a gig and came back in and relocked the door. It was a big one, like Neptune's trident, with a long sturdy handle. A wicked weapon, if you ever used it on anybody. I sat down on my couch with the gig close at hand. I was grimly determined to wait out the vigil, no matter how long it took.

I woke up on the couch at noon. Christy was blithely rattling pans in the kitchen. I felt slightly better, but shamefaced about sleeping. I went out there and herded her away from the window.

"What's the idea?"

"I got hungry. I'm a big girl. I need regular meals."

I noticed how she was dressed. She had on an old faded pair of my khaki shorts with the legs rolled high and tight, and a blue bath towel pinned into a halter.

"It was hot and I got comfortable," she said.

"Mmmm," I said.

"Please, sir."

She was slightly breathtaking. The smell of food was good. I said, "Look. We can't stay cooped up forever."

"And why not?"

"That's a good question I won't answer. I'm going to go

check with that Luffberry. Come on and let me out and lock the door after me."

"Won't he be mad?"

"I don't care much at this point."

I tested the door behind me to make certain it was locked. I yelled through to her to stay away from windows. I went down to her place, looking warily from side to side at the brush, feeling as though the shells underfoot were actually eggshells.

Luffberry was annoyed. And bored. As he was chewing me out, Elly came warily up to report a phone call for him. I waited for him. He came back in five minutes to report, sourly, that we could relax. After a lot of false starts the dogs had led the pursuit to a bay shore dock, that the owner of said dock thereupon reported a boat missing, and that the boat itself had been spotted pulled ashore on Horseshoe Key. The dogs had been transported there and had lost the trail when the fugutive had, apparently, taken to walking on the water. But he was, evidently, on Horseshoe Key which, Luffberry observed, was a plenty damn fool thing for a man in his spot to do, seeing as how there were only two bridges and thus two ways off it, both bridges now being blocked. He further observed that all this information had been available at eleven, and they had only now gotten around to informing him, and they desired his presence on Horseshoe Key and were sending a car for him at once.

"It proves to me, anyhow," Luffberry said, "that the guy is nuts."

I went back to my place. Christy let me in and said, "Lunch is on the table, master."

We sat and started to eat and I told her the news. She listened carefully and looked worried.

"Andy, love, wouldn't you say he was . . . intelligent?"

"In a twisted way."

"I keep thinking of what my father told me a long time ago when he took me to see Thurston, the magician. He told me never to watch the hand that waved around. Watch the other one."

"So?"

"That boat, Andy. It's too pat, isn't it? He's bright enough to know that Horseshoe Key is a trap. It would be . . . well, perfect for him if he had some way to get off Horseshoe Key. They'll all be watching the Key like a bunch of cats watching the wrong mousehole. I'm wondering if maybe you ought to lock the door again."

I looked at her for a good ten seconds. I got up and went and locked the door. Assumption: Kenney was no longer on the Key. How did he get off? Swim? A swimmer in the bay by daylight would be much too conspicuous. People just do not swim in the bay. But if a man were determined, and knew the tides, and knew the area well, he could go out the sand spit to Horseshoe Pass and swim across when the tide was dead low. I got up and looked at my tide chart. Dead low tide had come, this Tuesday morning, at nine forty-three. He could swim the neck of the pass, given a break in the way of no fishing boats around. And that would bring him out on Vera Key, the next one south from Horseshoe Key. He'd have five minutes to swim across before the tide began to swirl in from the Gulf, turbulent enough to drown him. An airplane would not be likely to spot a head in the water. The police would think in terms of a boat or a car, and, finding none missing, would start thrashing through the shrubbery, of which Horseshoe Key has plenty.

Once on Vera Key he would be two miles from the mainland. One mile and seven-eighths down a sand road down the center of the small key, and then a short narrow causeway with a wooden hump-backed bridge, and an old couple who lived in the bridge house and opened the bridge manually when it had to be turned to let a boat through.

Swim the pass at nine forty-three. Ten minutes to get to the bridge. Call it ten o'clock at the bridge.

I went over it for Christy. She was thoughtful. I told her what I had in mind. She became more thoughtful.

"Well," she said at last, "I guess they'd remember seeing him go over the bridge. It wouldn't hurt anything."

"It's an animal instinct to double back on your tracks, throw off pursuit. That guy has lived most of his life as something being hunted. And he knows the area. It would be as good a way as any. A hell of a lot more devious than taking the stolen boat south a way, but actually a hell of a lot more effective."

"It would be better than just sitting around here."

"O.K., then?"

"I guess . . . O.K., Andy."

"I'd rather have you with me than locked up here. I don't ever want you out of my sight again, Christy."

I went out cautiously, checked the area, moved the Cad closer to the door and opened the far door of the car. I honked and she came scuttling out, piled in and banged the door shut as I backed it around. I drove out our road, turned south on the trail and drove a fast five miles before turning right into the obscure little road that led to the Vera Key bridge. One day it won't be obscure. It will have become another fat rich Key, loaded with heavy money, homes out of the architectural magazines. Right now Vera Key is just a half step ahead of the bulldozers, but it is already too late to expect to come down and grab yourself good land and wait for the rise. The rise has happened, and the land is sewed up and the boys are waiting.

It was a mile in to the bridge. The bridge was open. Two big cars with northern plates were waiting. A fat, elderly, red-faced man stood indignantly in the sun with his hands on his hips, glaring at the bridge.

I looked up and down the channel and there wasn't a boat in sight. I got out and the indignant man turned on me as though I were personally responsible.

"I'm trying to get onto Vera Key to look at some land there, and by God, what kind of a way is this to run a goddamn bridge!"

"Shush!" his wife hissed at him from the car. "Shush!"

"You can bet your life I'm going to have something to say about a bunch of lazy crackers going away and leaving the bridge open. What the hell kind of a way is this to run a . . ."

"Shush!"

"Stop shushing me, dammit! I . . ." He looked beyond me and I saw the usual Hallowell reaction cut him off in mid stride and leave him with a wondering, enfeebled smile.

Christy came up beside me. "What is it, Andy?" The bridge tender's house was on the Vera Key side. It had an ominously silent look.

"There isn't anybody there," the man said. "I blew my horn until I was afraid my battery would run down."

I knew I wanted a look. The bridge was of the kind that turns on a central pier. It is turned by standing on the bridge itself and walking around and around with a big crank gadget, like an ox turning a millstone. When it is turned at right angles to its usual position, a boat can go through on either side of it. The crank affair was sticking up out of the socket in the bridge floor.

I walked over and looked at the gap. About twelve feet. I had no great urge to try to jump twelve feet and clear the bridge rail on the far side. The tide current was running in swift below me.

Down the bank to my left I saw an old skiff pulled up on shore without oars. But it did have a claw anchor tossed up into the brush at the end of about twenty feet of sturdy-looking rope. I went down and removed the anchor line from the bow, brought it back up.

"What are you going to do?" Christy asked.

"Just watch and cheer in the right places." I tossed the anchor over the bridge rail. It pulled free the first time. The second time it caught. I yanked on it hard, then fastened it to the front bumper of the car of the indignant citizen and got him to back up slowly until the line was taut.

I then went across it, hand over hand. It pulled my shoulders practically free of the sockets, and by the time I got both hands on the bridge rail, all I could do was hang there for a minute. Then I got my knee up, pulled myself up the rest of the way and climbed feebly over the rail.

I bowed and Christy clapped. I unhooked the anchor and tossed it back and over to one side, and Christy busied herself returning it to the skiff. I began to walk around and around pushing on the big crank and the bridge slowly returned to its normal position, coming to a jarring stop when it had turned as far as it should. I took the crank out and tossed it out of the way by the rail and trotted off the other end of the bridge.

Christy was right behind me when I found the bridge keeper and his wife. The old couple were on the floor, face-down, side by side. Their wrists were fastened behind them with leader wire, twisted cruelly tight. Their ankles were fastened in the same way. The pliers with which it had been done were close at hand. They had a cutting edge. I snipped the wire from her wrists and ankles first. She sat up at once and began to untie the rag tied around her mouth. Christy helped her up as I unsnipped the old man. He got the rag off his mouth and started cursing. Most of it, it seemed, was directed at some damn fool who sat over there the other side of the bridge and blew his damn fool horn until you couldn't hear yourself think. He went spryly out, rubbing his wrists, to inspect his precious bridge.

The old lady was willing to talk. Almost too willing.

"He come here around ten o'clock and he asked if we had bait, and he waited while George opened the bridge for a boat and closed it again, and while George was closing it, he came right in here and tied me up before I could hardly squeak. And then he got George when he came in. I swear he was like a crazy man. I heard him out in my kitchen, eating and talking to himself, like. And then a boat blew for the bridge to open, and he went on out and opened it himself. Then I heard some yelling and I heard the boat going off down the channel."

I told her he was a crazy man, a murderer, and she looked as if she might faint.

"Which way was the boat headed?"

"South."

I saw the telephone and told her I wanted to use it. I couldn't get Wargler or George. I got the young one they called Jimmy and told him and he said he'd get word to them out on the Key right away.

The old man was still cursing. I went outside with Christy.

"It's pretty obvious, now, Christy. He opened the bridge for a boat and then dropped onto the boat from the bridge and took over. The boat was headed south."

I called to the old man, "About what time did that boat go through?"

"Quarter to eleven. He hung around a while after he tied us up like he did."

By my watch it was nearly one-thirty. Two and three-quarter hours. Roy Kenney was still widening the gap. Assume fifteen knots. He could be nearly forty miles away in a straight line. Or he could have made the commandeered craft put him ashore at any number of places. He had moved so quickly and boldly and well, that it gave me the hopeless feeling he was going to get away.

From the air they could search for a cabin cruiser drifting someplace, or aground. Maybe the people aboard would be lucky, the way the old couple had been lucky. Spared by a whim.

There wasn't anything else we could do. With Christy beside me I drove slowly back toward Tickler Terrace. Out on the trail two police cars went by us headed in the opposite direction, sirens lusty. I caught a glimpse of Chief Wargler's florid face in the second car.

Nineteen

WARGLER STOPPED at four-thirty to tell us his troubles, and find out how I'd happened to go down to the bridge at Vera Key. He seemed depressed.

"By God, son, we've done about everything I can think of. Got four planes working now, checking every boat in a hundred mile area headed away from here. Pilots say the damn fools wave at them. Put an alert on the ship-to-shore. Even got that Air Force crash boat out of Sarasota working for us. Tying up all waterways traffic. Not a trace of the guy. This is going to look awful bad for me. I hate to think about it, even."

"He can't get away, though, can he?" Christy asked.

"There's one way I hate to think about, girl. Suppose he sees an empty dock. O.K. Herd the people below, kill 'em, tie up the boat and take off. And we can't check every cruiser tied up to a dock on the coast. He's had enough time, with luck, to be out of the state by now, if he's running. But I keep getting the funny feeling he's hanging around. Maybe it isn't so funny after all. He didn't have any money on him. He must have hid that forty thousand someplace. It would be nice to use it for running. Maybe he doesn't want to run. Maybe he wants to wait for it to get dark and start killing some more people."

Christy shuddered. "Hey! Cut it out."

"You can't figure those crazy people. They play God. Our rules don't mean a damn to them. Well, I'm going back to see what's happening, if anything."

He drove off. With all that talk about darkness, daylight seemed very precious. And there didn't seem to be enough of it left. Not nearly enough. If he was still loose at dusk, I was going to take Christy into town and ask to have her put in a cell.

We wandered aimlessly down to the bank of the creek and out to the mouth of it where it flows into the bay. It was as good a place as any, because we were on fairly open land there, the brush way behind us. Some trout fishermen were circling slowly in the flats, over the weeds. One of the commercial fishermen went by straining his eyes to spot the surface whirls that mullet make.

"I just wish it was over," Christy said. "If he gets away I'll never . . . really feel safe again."

The channel curves to within twenty yards of the mouth of the creek before cutting back out into the center of the bay. A cruiser came slowly down the channel with two girls in bright skimpy clothes sitting in the trolling chairs, rods over the stern. I put my arm around Christy.

"They'll get him."

"Gosh, I hope so."

I wondered vaguely what the girls were after, trolling down the channel. Reds, maybe. But the rods looked a bit hefty for that. And they weren't working the rods at all. And then, far behind the cruiser I saw an unweighted spoon prancing foolishly on top of the water. Anybody that stupid, I decided, doesn't deserve a fish. A hell of a waste of a nice big mahogany cruiser, about twenty-eight foot. The girls looked like store window dummies, the way they were sitting, as though heat and monotony had paralyzed them.

Maybe part of it was the ridiculous demonstration of how not to fish. And part of it could have been their very rigidity. But the metallic glint from the shadow of the cabin overhang brought it all into focus. It froze me for one tenth of one unbelievable second, and then I grabbed Christy's wrist and nearly yanked her arm off. She let out a startled yelp punctured by a flat crackling sound that came across the water. I wasted no time looking back. Christy caught panic from me and did her share of running and zigging and zagging until we crashed, stumbling and falling, into the delightful brush. There was another crack and something that whipped through the leaves. I rolled over and over, shoving her ahead of me.

Beyond the fringe of brush we scrambled up again and headed for my house. I dared then, to turn and look back, just in time to see Roy Kenney in smeared white shirt and khaki pants climb on top of the cabin roof, rifle in his hand. A twenty-two, from the sound of it. He stared toward us, and I shoved Christy around a corner of the house. The cruiser rocked then, oddly, and came to a stop, staggering Kenney a bit. He turned and yelled down at whoever was at the wheel. They had gone aground and Roy, for a while, had lost interest in pot-shooting.

He was a pleasant target against the blue late afternoon sky. I went into the garage and grabbed the big spinning outfit. Eight feet of glass surf-casting rod, with a big Rumer Atlantic spanning reel carrying three hundred yards of fifteen pound monofilament. It is a luxury I bought myself, and I use it for tarpon and kings. That character silhouetted against the sky, yelling and waving his arms, had taken a shot at my lady. He had tried to choke her and drown her.

The rod was rigged with a big number six Reflecto spoon, and a heavy rudder sinker a foot from the spoon, wire leader connecting them. I had used it last for surf casting when the kings were running close off shore.

The cruiser was grunting and straining in full reverse. Christy gave a despairing cry as I ran out with the rod in my hand. I ran down to the open place near where we were first standing. Roy Kenney had his back to me. He was bent forward a bit from the waist, peering down at the bow where the craft had gone aground. I could read the name on her. *The Sea Flight,* out of Tampa.

I didn't know how soon he would turn. I took the line off the pickup, hooked it around my finger and swung back. I knew I could reach the distance easily. I was used to the rod and the line and that particular amount of weight and what I could do with it.

I let go, ready to turn and run like a rabbit if it was a bad cast. The big spoon twinkled in a high arc, the line bellying after it. I saw Kenney straighten up. I saw then that it was in a perfect line, but too far beyond him. I nipped the flowing line with my finger, and hooked the line onto the manual pickup. I saw the twinkling spoon fall over his shoulder, fall in front of him, and as it did so, I reared back and set the hook with a hard slanting swing of the big glass rod.

There is never any doubt when you set a hook. There is either resistance or there isn't. I hit something solid. I saw arms flail wildly, saw the rifle fly, saw the man stagger backward off the edge of the cabin roof and fall into the water with a mighty splash, completely missing the narrow catwalk around the cabin.

He came up, and he splashed and struggled and took some line. Not the clean, good, thrilling run of a tough fish, but a few nasty, dull little tugs. I kept pressure on him. He tried to turn back to the cruiser but I swung him around and began to reel him in. He had the same inertness as a big grouper after the first hard effort to get free. His arms splashed at the water.

"Come on, baby," I said softly, reeling. "Come on to daddy."

He had not made a sound. He stopped struggling. I kept the rod tip high so he wouldn't foul against the bottom. He came in oddly docile. He came in and there was a spreading red stain in the water. I could see the two girls and a man standing on the cruiser, staring at me. There was too much red in the water. I went down the bank. He was on his back. His eyes were half open. The big spoon lay across his throat.

The barb had gone into the side of his throat. His struggles had torn the wound a bit too deep. I threw the rod up the bank, got his wrists and dragged the body up onto the bank. And then I went over a little way and I was sick. There was no end to being sick. The worst, perhaps, was, that with the life out of him, that flat sheen of evil was gone. And he was just a youngish man, dead, with a face you would not notice twice, with brown hair, with one button on the white shirt that did not match the others, with the pores of his cheeks a bit enlarged, and accented by the slant of the late sun. Death is a word. It is in every issue of every newspaper. It is in the slap-dash novels, casual as cornflakes, with the cool-eyed young hero looking with satisfaction at the corpse, reholstering the trusty weapon.

I was sick, and when I got over that I couldn't look at it there on the bank, and I wanted to laugh and cry at the same time. It was a grotesquerie, and an abrupt distortion and dislocation of the soul. I couldn't get a crazy picture out of the back of my mind. Me, standing for the camera, with rod and smile, and that thing on the bank hung up by the heels.

I knew that Christy was close by me. And I knew that helped.

There was a lot of unreality about the next few days. Once the two girls and the man on the cruiser had been quieted down, they were able to tell how Roy Kenney had dropped onto the boat, how there had been something in his face that made any thought of resistance impossible and implausible. The twenty-two rifle had been aboard, for their standard game of plinking empty beer cans out in the Gulf.

They told how he had directed them around the south end of Vera Key and back north through the Gulf. Three times he had tried to head north, but had been forced to swing slowly back as the search planes came close and low. He had crouched back in the protection of the cabin, forcing the two girls to smile and wave and pretend to troll. And he spoke endlessly at last of going back to "get" somebody. They had headed back into the bay and he had made them troll up and down, up and down the channel off the creek, until finally the man and girl had appeared on the shore and he had fired at them, so shocking him that he had inadvertently run the cruiser aground at the side of the narrow channel.

An adventure magazine signed them up for a ghost written article, and a brisk-talking man tried to make the same deal with me, calling it a "natural," but all I wanted to do was try to forget that long slow-motion time of the silver spoon twinkling in the air, dropping toward the man on the cabin roof. The wire service gave it fat coverage, and I was an unwilling national celebrity for all of two days. And I couldn't go out on the street without running into the clumsiest, crudest jokes imaginable. The first time that happened I went back and took the rod and reel and heaved the whole rig as far out into the bay as I could manage, and turned away without even waiting to see it hit.

In all of it, Christy was the only one who seemed to understand.

Electric shock therapy brought Joy Kenney out of it. They tell me she looked forty when she was released, and went away. Steve told me what she said. Roy had told her about a man named John Long who, if he found out something, would very dearly want to kill him, and probably would try to. And later he told her that John Long had the evidence he wanted, and that Long's wife had been careless, and that he had an idea John Long had found where he was living by following Mary Eleanor. She told them all this, Steve said, in a flat gray hopeless voice. It had been one of those improbable coincidences that always seem to be happening that got her into John Long's office. She thought that would give her a chance to warn Roy or help him, and maybe a chance, she thought, to talk John Long out of too violent an answer to adultery.

And Steve said it was a good guess that John Long had studied the cut-out pictures of Roy's face so thoroughly that he immediately saw the resemblance between Roy and Joy, and I had witnessed his momentary confusion. The cut-out heads, by the way, were recovered from a Miami firm of investigators.

George got his stolid mind set on the missing money. He plodded in and took Roy's gray car apart. Then he took the shack apart. Then he took the island apart. He found the forty thousand and the negatives and another set of prints, unmutilated, in a wide-top gallon glass jar, made waterproof and lashed to mangrove roots below the low tide mark fifty feet from the shack. And in finding the money, they found out a little bit more—or perhaps a little bit less—about the way Roy Kenney's mind worked. More than half the money had been cut up with scissors. He had cut little lewd clever twisted paper silhouettes, contorted mannikins, out of the money. They showed considerable artistic talent, and obviously represented many hours of work. In an odd way, there was an inevitability about it; it was perhaps the ultimate violation of one of our gods, a god that Kenney refused to do homage to.

How the pictures were taken, and when, and by whom, were never discovered.

The grotesque death I had caused had made something gray happen to me, and Christy seemed to understand.

I couldn't seem to rise off the ground. Then the next Saturday came along, and in midafternoon there was a booming rain that lasted fifteen minutes, and left the air washed and clean and clear. I'd been at meetings most of the day, and it was settled as to how we'd go ahead with Key Estates starting on Monday. I got my car back that day, with a complete new motor, and I drove back to my place and Christy was sitting again on her steps. The sun was on her and she was brown and she wore skimpy shorts and narrow halter, both in white with dime-sized red polka dots. I stopped and she came to the car and put her hands on the door and yanked them back. "Ouch!"

"You always do that."

"I'm a dull girl. But I know what day it is. Saturday."

"And Wilburt is getting along without you?"

"To a limited extent." She stared at me and I looked back for long seconds, and we both looked away at the same instant. "Andy?"

"It *is* Saturday."

"Where were we, Andy, when we were so rudely interrupted?" I looked at her cheek and saw a faint redness under the tan and knew what that cost her in pride, and it made me a little ashamed.

"The sensible thing to do is to backtrack. Re-create the mood. Wear the blue, Christy."

There was gladness in her eyes. "Give me . . . forty minutes."

I drove to my place, laid out fresh clothes. I showered and while I was under the spray I thought of how it would be, how it would very definitely be. We would drive to Sarasota, and the copper mugs would be chill, and Charlie Davies would play "Penthouse," which is indeed a very fine thing, and on the way back the top would be down and there would be a ridiculous number of stars and she would sit close beside me, and light my cigarettes for me, my big blonde with warm night wind in her hair.

And something inside me, something that had been dragging me down, beat its wings hard enough to get off the ground, and then began to fly very well indeed. I out-roared the water with "Shortnin' Bread" and remembered, sort of all at once, that I was that guy . . . that fella shot with luck, that superbly happy jerk named Andrew Hale McClintock.

About the Author

JOHN D. MACDONALD was an American novelist and short story writer. His works include the Travis McGee series and the novel *The Executioners,* which was adapted into the film *Cape Fear.* In 1962 MacDonald was named a Grand Master of the Mystery Writers of America; in 1980 he won a National Book Award. In print he delighted in smashing the bad guys, deflating the pompous, and exposing the venal. In life he was a truly empathetic man; his friends, family, and colleagues found him to be loyal, generous, and practical. In business he was fastidiously ethical. About being a writer, he once expressed with gleeful astonishment, "They pay me to do this! They don't realize, I would pay them." He spent the later part of his life in Florida with his wife and son. He died in 1986.

Made in the USA
Middletown, DE
03 July 2024

56781646R00144